Joe's Tap

The Story of Maurine and
Tales of the Other Cape May

Joe's Tap
The Story of Maurine and Tales of the Other Cape May

Copyright © 2016 by K. Lee Washington

This is a work of fiction. All of the characters, names, incidents, organizations, and dialogue in this novel are either the products of the author's imagination or are used fictitiously.

iUniverse books may be ordered through booksellers or by contacting:

iUniverse
1663 Liberty Drive
Bloomington, IN 47403
www.iuniverse.com
1-800-Authors (1-800-288-4677)

ISBN: 978-1-4759-5127-1 (sc)
ISBN: 978-1-4759-5128-8 (hc)
ISBN: 978-1-4759-5129-5 (e)

Library of Congress Control Number: 2012917498

Print information available on the last page.

iUniverse rev. date: 08/10/2016

Acknowledgements

Special thanks to childhood friends Mrs. Elizabeth M. Grant and Dr. La Netta Hammill for their adult contribution and much needed encouragement to make this book happen. Also thanks to Dr. Debra Ihunnah for her support.

Prologue

white foam on the beer
retreated to the ages
like this morning's tide....

> The *Cape May Herald* campaigned during 1901 to remove African-American residents from Cape May City. Marcus Scull, the newspaper's editor, who owned property along an African-American section of Lafayette Street, printed lurid accounts of Cape May City's "colored population" who allegedly loitered about Lafayette Street drinking heavily and insulting white vacationers as they passed by in their fine carriages. The *Herald* insisted that Cape May City could never return to the glories of pre-Civil War days until the community rid itself of its African-American population. Scull published a letter on the front page of his newspaper from a reader who wanted to make Lafayette Street "an attractive avenue for settlement by white families" and "free from mixture with the colored population which now chiefly occupy the avenue for some distance north of Franklin Street, with gas works and all things else objectionable removed farther back toward the creek to another locality."
>
> This passage was reprinted from Jeffery M. Dorwart's book, *Cape May County, New Jersey.* Rutgers University Press, 1992. Page 172.

Joe's Tap is a chronologically layered, fictional account, about Cape May balancing its responsibility in a democracy and still trying to hang on to a pre-Civil War state of mind. This mind-set founded in the earliest days of America's establishment was that whites and blacks maintain differing social plateaus. Some institutions in America were quick to move forward, serving all of its citizens on an equal basis. Even through today, some parties have not come to grips with America as a multi-ethnic civilization. Others expeditiously erased their "problem" by hiding under contrived bureaucratic ploys.

From post-World War II America, into the infancy of the 21st century, the United States faced numerous challenges to its identity and objectives. In Cape May, Joe's Tap brought together philosophies that might pave the way for America to have a more just direction. The only catch was that one needed a few drinks to make those connections.

Behind the scenes at Joe's Tap was a little girl who was powerless to combat her own un-civil rights. *Joe's Tap* explains that girl's rise from an unfortunate upbringing to a belated opportunity to find happiness.

The story of *Joe's Tap* borrows much of the attitude that existed in the Dorwart passage. Beyond that, *Joe's Tap* is a fictional account of how some of this could have been accomplished. The identities of any of the characters included in this story are also fictional. If they evoke the image of someone you may have heard of or known is strictly coincidental. *Joe's Tap's* function is to focus on Cape May in the second half of the 20th century and the relationships that could have happened and provides the backdrop for the "other" Cape May.

Chapter One *Joe's Tap*

The distinct sound of bar stools being knocked over and the jangling of beer bottles broken in vengeful fury were featured characteristics of discord when the fishermen hit Joe's Tap. A wayward projectile, disguised as a customer, would bump into the treasured jukebox and the needle would scratch the spinning record. Men marking out territory would clash over female association. Drunkenness was not an alien behavior pattern around a saloon. Many times this had to do with the black guys not appreciating the Puerto Rican guys having the where-with-all to be seductive with the local girls. Joe's Tap had fights for other reasons as well, but the fishermen seemed to bring the pugnacious best out of the local wolves on the prowl. In the area around Joe's Tap, its history had been marked by alcohol-induced confrontations and that never sat well with the establishment's idea of a first-class resort town.

When fishermen would get time off in port towns, sporting a wallet filled with dollars from a bountiful catch, they would venture into those harbor towns. On Cape Island/Cape May, Joe's Tap was the place for men of color to get a drink, and maybe find a woman to spend some time. The Puerto Rican fishermen were young, virile, and enchanting. They weren't totally white, and they weren't classically black. This presented a murky view of cataloging where they "belonged." In mid-20th century Cape Island, there was generally no in-between. Their English was poor. This added a spark of mystery to their presence, and openly hampered communication. They did not possess *Mayflower* roots from which some Cape Islanders could proudly trace their lineage. They spent money. Their entry into the bar bloated the number of ready, willing, and vocal males vying for the limited pool of Cape Island girls. Bar owners Joe and Mary Di Cicco had to restore order from inevitable conflicts before the bedlam brought avid constabulary and undermined their business.

As Cape Island was in a period of distinct change, so was America, and so too was Joe's Tap. Joe's Tap finally got a television in 1959. Maybe a step late in catching up to the rest of America. The TV at Joe's Tap stayed on top of the evolving news and sports of the day, even when the jukebox was in full torque. This was the advent of the Age of Camelot, the espoused heraldic period of America where a youthful messenger brought forth optimism and good news. President John F. Kennedy, a Roman Catholic, was that exalted messenger. As the picture on Joe's TV was in black and white, hence, much of the news on which it focused, tinged socially and politically in black and white.

The regulars in Joe's Tap were a hodgepodge of local citizenry who could interpret a perfectly simple concept and, by evening's end, have everything totally screwed up. They followed the March on Washington, in August of 1963. Many of them observed the unfolding of President Kennedy's demoralizing assassination and funeral, right from their seat in Joe's Tap. The theme of conversation and debate usually centered on how these events would impact on the lives of African-Americans.

African-Americans were taking steps to become a more stable participant in the American system. The people in the bar could be a pretty intimidating set of pseudo-intellectuals banding together to settle the disputes of civil rights, stopping the advance of communism or defining whether Jesse Owens could beat Bob Hayes. Luckily they did not take their less than researched opinions too seriously. The cohesive theme of their union was that they could relax and get away from job or family issues at Joe's Tap.

The inauspicious March 1962 storm and its aftermath was one of the few periods that brought a consensus of unification of spirit from the patrons. Its consequences continued them on a path of questioning how they would be affected from the rebuilding of the town to whether they would have jobs.

The regulars of Joe's Tap were a social club with no dues and had no scheduled meetings. The members were generally men of color who were born during the William Howard Taft-Woodrow Wilson administrations. There were no vocational or educational obstacles. They ranged from grade school dropouts to a couple with some college credits. In the summer, the regular corps would expand with vacationing school teachers from Philadelphia or Baltimore being around. The level of education would elevate with the teachers, but not necessarily the content or intensity of the debates. Some never sought a drink, just a forum and an audience. Of course women frequented the bar and were just as diverse and outspoken as the guys, but as regulars were fewer in number.

There were colorful personalities with equally colorful nicknames, and each with a story to tell, or the insight and predisposition to denounce someone else's. There was Major, General, Judge, and Doc. There was Big Dick (not to be confused with Blue Dick), Puerto Rican Jesus, Greenie, Clarkie, and Mr. Sid.

Big Dick's real name was Richard Gray, who was six-feet-five and weighed 270 pounds. Blue Dick's name was Richard Blue; he stood five-feet-seven and weighed 155. It was pretty easy to give Big Dick his name. But nobody thought it was fair, or had the guts to call Blue Dick, "Little Dick"! "Little Richard" was already in use in the 1950s. There was also Jinx.

Jinx was white. Jinx offered a contrarian view in Joe's Tap to the tirade that white people were "the root of all evil." When in Joe's Tap, he had to carry the banner of Caucasianality and take the hits from his black brethren. Joe was perceptive enough to let the regulars have their say without inflicting his opinions that might work against business. He participated, but counted his words and left Jinx to define an off-brand sociology.

Back in 1957, Jinx supported the postulate that Mickey Mantle was better than Willie Mays. The Mays faction slaughtered Jinx, the sole Mantle guy, even though Mickey had won a Triple Crown the year before and his second MVP in a row that year. Jinx struck out swinging when he went to bat on behalf of Mantle. This was a minority position of severe dimension in Joe's Tap. Jinx was always out-manned, but not necessarily out-smarted.

Jinx grew up poor in South Carolina, came to Cape May in the 1930s while stationed there at the naval facility as a dirigible mechanic and stayed. He talked with a drawl, which enhanced his agitating perspectives. Jinx never married, but he had lived with a black woman since 1940, and was a Joe's Tap charter regular. It established Jinx as a friendly adversary, a foil, and one of the guys. Jinx was victimized by a malady that some of the black guys had too, alcoholism.

Jinx's usual verbal sparring partner in the bar was Doc. Doc and Jinx would drink together even when they were not inside the bar. Doc was a legendary high school athlete whose rise to loftier echelons of sports fame in college was undone by the advent of World War II. His time in Europe was spent dodging German mortar shells and learning the intricacies of French wine. When he returned home in 1946, he had an acute nervous disorder and a full-fledged drinking problem. He was unable to maintain a job. To get by, he worked as a day-hire on the ice wagon in the summers. Jinx was ten years older than Doc, but the two had fused a relationship that included reading newspapers and debating the issues of the day. They drank whichever spirits they could get their hands on. If alcohol had been eliminated from the equation, both Doc and Jinx should have advanced much further in life than glued to a stool at Joe's.

Following the dramatic March on Washington, the unsettling assassination of President Kennedy and during President Johnson's term, civil rights legislation was passed by Congress and enacted by the president that focused on the improvement of minorities as citizens. President Kennedy's brother Robert, who was attorney general until Johnson's Cabinet was installed in 1965, led the charge of implementing the changes. The Civil Rights Act of 1964 prohibited discrimination in voting, among other things, which should be part of customary democratic practice.

Although Cape Island was unequivocally integrated, the Civil Rights Act was not met with a warm reception in many segments of America. In southern states, much resistance followed this law and television captured history in the making. The topic in Joe's Tap turned to the atrocious sight of African-Americans being beaten in Selma, Alabama, during the turn into spring of 1965. Their issue was that most basic order of a democracy, the right to vote. State troopers with vicious dogs chased and battered black people who were trying to register to vote, trying to be American.

On a slow spring evening in the middle of the week, the regulars were evaluating the beatings in Alabama. All of them were agitated about it. Mo and Mary sat at the other end of the bar not paying heed to the talk, while Joe manned the bar by himself. "I was in Tuskegee during the war. I never left the airfield. Guys who had been in town told me what those rednecks do," said Greenie, who was hacking and coughing in between habitual puffs on an un-filtered Chesterfield cigarette. "They would beat up black guys for fun, and the cops wouldn't do nothing."

"Aw man, you was never in no service. You didn't get out of prison until '46," insisted Judge who was in his mid-fifties, and had protruding gray eyebrows. "I know 'cause I was in the courthouse when they sent your ass away."

"You senile fool, that was my cousin. And he was only in the joint for six months in 1947. You're the reason they don't let us vote. You're an imbecile!" Greenie charged. "Plus you never was no judge, you was just the damn custodian. We ought to call you Janitor instead of Judge!"

"Do you know that there were no black people in prison before 1865?" Doc asked to no one in particular. "Then after the Civil War ended they just started to round up black people, charge them with a crime, convict them, and sentence them to slavery as their punishment for as long as they wanted to keep them. Blacks were required to do the same stuff they did before slavery was abolished. The mess going on now is just an extension of that slavery shit."

"Hey Joe, I bet if you sent Benito to Alabama he'd kick those punk-ass dogs' asses!" Major asserted. Benito was the huge collie asleep on the floor next to the bar.

"You're damn right! You remember when we had that fight in here and the cops brought their shepherd? They still got that dog?

Well, Benito made that dog back down when that cop came toward Mo. Hell, Mo didn't do nothing. He just happened to, you know, be black!" Joe offered.

"Hey, Senor Joe, somebody call the cops and say that blacks and Puerto Ricans fight. We just had an argument over whether some guy don't pay his bet on a pool shot," claimed diminutive Puerto Rican Jesus. Closer to the truth was that Puerto Rican Jesus, who had the physical dimensions of a thoroughbred jockey and had doggedly immobilized a much larger guy in a headlock, was trying to squeeze the money out of him after the player failed to pay off on the lost bet.

Puerto Rican Jesus's taproom identity was a redundancy of ethnic delineation. Puerto Rican Jesus had a definite, dark olive, Latin physicality. He sported a trimmed beard, and shoulder-length straight black hair. His name was typically pronounced a Spanish "hey -sooce," except in the bar, where it embellished a Biblical intonation, "gee-sus." The only things in common between the two Jesuses were that they both toiled as journeymen carpenters, and spoke another language better than English.

Puerto Rican Jesus was one of the few Puerto Ricans to settle in Cape May following their stints on the fishing boats. The docked boat on which he worked broke away from its moorings and slammed into another docked boat during the infamous March 1962 storm and was immobilized. Jesus was stranded in Cape May, and never left. He had evolved into being an accepted regular of Joe's Tap after consistent hazing. As his English improved, he was able to counter barbed comments with his own repartee. His penchant for not backing down and his generally pleasant nature allowed him to mix with the regulars. Pointed comments about his background were fewer than they used to be. Those wanting to zing Puerto Rican Jesus had better be able to handle his comeback. Additionally, Puerto Rican Jesus's stature grew with a couple of bar battles where he showed his tenacity. The one that made the greatest impression was when he promised to stick a guy in the ribs with a shiny switchblade knife that he produced. Most importantly Jesus seemed like he was poised to carry out his threat. Guys decided not to make Puerto Rican Jesus the butt of their bar humor anymore.

"That's right! Well I think Mary got a little nervous and called the cops," recalled Joe. "They came in here and just started swinging night sticks. Benito chased everybody out of here."

Big Dick added, "Puerto Rican Jesus got busted in the head that night by another Puerto Rican guy. Remember that Jesus?" By now, all of the regulars are picking their own brains to remember, without particular emphasis on truthful precision, about that scrum at Joe's Tap.

"Si, Senor Big Dick, I winning fight, too! But it not with Puerto Rican. It was colored guy from Camden; he didn't pay me! Somebody heet me with bottle or nightstick. I no remember after that."

"Fellas, let me tell ya, we gotta stop fighting and pay attention to what's going on, man! My great-grandmother was a slave in Mississippi. She told me what life was like back then, and that is about the same stuff you saw on that television," Mr. Sid said, as he tugged his sweat-stained cap for emphasis. "America ain't changed in a hundred years! Damn it, I agree with Doc."

"Mr. Sid, do you vote?" Clarkie asked.

"I'd vote, but I never signed up," said Mr. Sid.

"See Sid, that's the problem. We got black folks in America getting eaten by dogs and white folks, and you ain't even registered. We got folks collecting welfare and unemployment who aren't even registered. That ain't right! You got no excuses if you're not registered," blasted Clarkie. "We can vote here in Cape May, so vote!"

"Vote hell, I can't even read! Kennedy could read. Lincoln could read. That Malcolm X could read, and somebody shot his ass last month. Like to see him read his way out of that one!" Mr. Sid concluded with a couple hat tugs, with gusto.

"He died so black folks like you wouldn't have to take those handouts you get down on Montpelier Avenue," claimed Major. The guys laugh at Major's kidding Mr. Sid. Ironically, almost all of them have a personal white "sugar-daddy" in the Montpelier Avenue area. This is where the heart of Victorian Cape May pulsed. They don't want to get too vociferous about following up and exposing their own sensitive nerve.

To and from the homes and yards around Montpelier Avenue, men like Mr. Sid and Big Dick pushed two-wheeled carts that contained their rakes, shovels, hoes, and lawn mowers; crucial documents that validated a black man's necessity in that part of town. The lawn mowers were manually operated, with forward churning blades. Most of these guys at the bar had cut grass in that area. Most of them walked to their accounts.

Walking was still the most expeditious way to get around Cape May for the regulars. Among all of the regulars, few owned automobiles. Puerto Rican Jesus rode a bicycle. Greenie had a well-used 1947 Ford pick-up truck that he used for trash removal. While Greenie unloaded his truck at the dump, the sea gulls gathered around thinking that the smell presented a potential meal on wheels; a movable feast, although rarely it did. Everyone knew when Greenie was nearing by the surge of squawking gulls winding their way through the streets. As he parked his truck the birds would hover and investigate, usually in disappointment. The distinct aroma of his truck, over and over again, proved more fruitful than any food discovered. Yet the seagulls persisted in their surveillance.

On this night eight guys were in the bar. The jukebox was uncharacteristically still. Joe was not being tested because the regulars were not big spenders. They were eagerly thirsting for understanding about the situation in Alabama, and united in their confusion about its resolution.

"Hey Jinx, you vote?" Clarkie asked.

"Damn right! I voted for Goldwater because he was going to stick a bomb up the Rusky's butts," replied Jinx.

"What's that going to prove? Then we get stuck with one up our ass and we'll look like Hiroshima, or worse than that, North Philly or Camden," Doc exaggerated. "What's that got to do with dogs in Alabama, anyway?"

"Hell, I don't know. I just know I ain't colored!" Jinx proffered.

"Amen to that," said Mr. Sid with a hat tug.

"Jinx, you're too stupid to be white!" Joe needled.

"Yeah Jinx, dawns on me that you're too stupid to be colored," goaded Clarkie.

Doc said, "Jinx is too stupid to be Benito!"

Amid the laughter and the liquor, Jinx sat there poised and ready. He pretty much endured these attacks any time race came up, which was all the time.

"Doc, why don't you go visit that Wizard of Oz and get yourself a brain? I might be stupid, but I was worth $100,000 more than you guys the day I was born. So you smart sons of bitches think on that!" Jinx challenged.

"Jinx you might be right, I don't even know what a silver spoon looks like. But nobody in here, if he had that much money, is stupid enough to drink it away in Joe's Tap like you do…Joe get me another Rheingold draft!" Big Dick ordered, as he was the only one re-filling his glass.

"Believe me, I've never had no silver spoon; I had to work. But I know that the jobs I got would be better than the ones you got. How many of you ever had a black boss?" The guys look around at each other without saying anything. "See no matter what job I had, I knew that if colored guys were working, I'd be the boss!"

"Jinx you certainly don't need a voting rights bill, you better hope Congress tries to stamp out learning disabilities; you occupy the meniscus on the learning curve. That is the only way for you to get cleared up of the problem you got. Maybe you ought to take that hundred grand you sleep on and use it to upgrade your common sense," clamored Doc. "You come up with the most con-vo-lut-ed bull-shit in this time zone!" Doc ranted, punctuating almost every syllable he spoke.

"Well Doc, I am not sure what a meniscus looks like, but if I were you, I'd look right here for it." Jinx grabbed his crotch.

"See, the more you talk, the more you prove my point!" Doc smugly exclaimed.

Susie McHendry and Bertha Fowler were two of the women regulars at Joe's Tap. They were childhood friends now in their mid-40s and worked together as cooks in a hotel. Susie's nickname was "Poison Sumac" because her name lent itself to the acid tongue she so easily used in Joe's. The large-busted Bertha was her drinking partner, and designated driver, even after they both had been drinking, especially since Bertha was the only one with a car. Both women had raised families and endured husbands of questionable domestic participation. They also avoided their home situations as much as possible.

Poison Sumac's husband had divided his attention between a girlfriend in Wildwood and being with his Cape May family, for a long time. They were the parents of five, now grown, children. Susie had resigned herself to this arrangement, noting few exits. Once she found out about the girlfriend, she was not willing to make him get out. This was a condition that she tolerated for over twenty years. She reasoned that she was better off with a part-time man, than no man at all. She spent considerable time in Joe's consoling herself, usually with shots of Absolut vodka.

Bertha lost her husband after fifteen years of marriage when the overloaded fishing boat, on which he worked, went down in a storm. She finished raising her three children by herself, and began spending time in Joe's Tap. The loneliness of being a widow combined with a limited number of desirable suitors chased Bertha into a marriage with another fisherman, whom she met at Joe's Tap involving some bizarre circumstances.

In the back yard of Joe's Tap stood a functioning, two-seat outhouse. It was generally never used, as Joe's had up-to-date indoor plumbing. One evening as the fisherman was wooing Bertha and their connection was reaching a fever pitch, he led Bertha from the bar through a back door, and away from Benito. They avidly entered the wooden structure for their own lustful indulgence. Not paying attention to the smell or the fact that there was no working light, they proceeded to evoke all of the passion and sexual aggression they could muster. They were animated, loud, and wrestled around in their own stinky love nest. Amid their wildly pointed sex program, and as both the fisherman and Bertha were large people and drunk, their girth was too much for the ancient john. After repeated bumping into the front wall, the fisherman had Bertha pinned against the wall and lost his balance as he went for her. His misstep took himself and Bertha hard into the wall and beyond. Their size over-powered the flimsy building, and it collapsed. It also woke up a snoozing Benito.

Next to the uneven pile of planks, boards, exposed nails and two-by-fours, an aroused Benito barked and bared his teeth. Bertha was screaming from Benito's snarling and the shock of one moment of being in the throes of physical romance and the next being in the back yard of Joe's Tap with barely anything on and the whole neighborhood investigating a major commotion.

It took Mo ten minutes to bulldoze the debris and put it in his truck, the next morning. He brought a truck load of clean soil when he came home that evening to fill on the hole. Mary had the girls plant the new plot with tulip and hyacinth bulbs. She had them rim the garden bed with yellow and purple crocuses. Although the calamity of this event brought much attention to Bertha from the regulars, she remained one of the gang without much amendment.

Once they were married, the initial charm and perceived devotion this man showered on Bertha proved to be a sham. He was a physically abusive alcoholic and pummeled Bertha one too many times. She came home from an evening of drinking at Joe's Tap and shot him twice, with a pistol she carried in her purse. He did not die, but she made her point. There was enough proof of his beating her that she did not have to do prison time. He found it in his best interest to find other quarters to reside, and moved out of town.

As part of her probation, she could not go into bars. For two years she did not enter Joe's Tap or any other saloon. After fulfilling the conditions of her sentence, Bertha spent more time in Joe's Tap with the vulgar and amusing Poison Sumac. Bertha's divorce was still in the works, but she was looking for love. Bertha's demeanor was the less boisterous of the two, but provided for a perfect symbiotic pairing with her outspoken pal.

Chapter Two *Cape Island*

R acism exposed its duplicitous face in some peculiar ways in Cape May during the 1950s and 1960s. Joe's Tap had more than a few fights regarding one's ethnicity. Not all of it was on a black and white theme. The play and subsequent movie *West Side Story* illustrated problems that Puerto Ricans moving into neighborhoods of New York City found during the fifties. The play was a capsulated rendition of the resentment and antagonism that built while the tenuous complexion of ethnic permanence darkened in an American community. Cape May bore such resentment.

Cape May proclaimed itself the Nation's Oldest Seashore Resort. It rested on the southern tip of New Jersey. It accepted life and buried its dead much like it had done for the previous three and a half centuries. Cape May had a reason for being there, just as the Atlantic Ocean had always been there. For all of the coastline on the Atlantic, the mere three miles of Cape May had been in use for as long as any in America, for relaxation and play.

The Atlantic supplied Cape May with a moderate climate, a natural salt air presence, and an understated allure that was addicting and profitable. In combination with the laws of Mother Nature, and monies to refurbish communities, Cape May evolved from being a listless, aging, semi-southern town to a sophisticated vacation spa. Its commercial profile touted remodeled and enhanced houses. These large homes were built during the mid-to-late 1800s. Queen Victoria reigned as sovereign of Great Britain during that time, and lent her name to the era's architecture.

Cape May did its best to confront radical changes to its profile and to re-direct its muddled destiny. The divisive national Civil War had consumed the American and Cape May consciousness less than one hundred years before. With the Emancipation Proclamation and the ultimate Union victory, people of African descent were led to think that they were free to enjoin in the liberties, as written in the U.S. Constitution. Positive socio-political efforts during Reconstruction were methodically dismantled by "separate but equal" racism (*Plessy v Ferguson*, 1896), and showed 20th century America as having distinct racial parameters that failed to approach constituted standards, and fair play. This High Court decision held that as long as black citizens had similar facilities as white people that American life was equitable. The sad distinction was that equality was meted out in disproportionate countenance. America showed that it manipulated its rules based on the color of a man's skin.

Following the *Plessy* decision, turn of the century attention focused on the negative reflection blacks presumably cast from the town. In the early 1900s, existing sentiment and published editorials by white businessmen openly discussed removing blacks from Cape May.

The overall contention was that blacks loitered, were boorish drunkards, and were not the welcoming committee the city wanted to extend to the region. A movement emerged to develop a community for black people (Whitesboro, N.J.) away from the sight lines of its fine white visitors. And because of the Supreme Court decision, this was thought to be an allowable and appropriate step. This black town was created. But possibly due to the imposing need for domestic workers, Cape May never lost its core black population; until 70 years later.

Former slaves and their offspring did not get the memo that their citizenship was indefinitely put on hold, and bit by bit sought to find out why that was. Cape May had a defined black section of town, as well as a portion of beach that was "devoted" to black beach-goers. One beach was consistently staffed with black lifeguards, and serviced by a black concessionaire. Many blacks questioned the social inequities of their existence. They had limited education, little economic base, and even less political clout to ignite desired corrections. African-Americans were customarily the cooks, domestics, and caretakers of white people's properties. Independent black businessmen did much of the landscaping. Oddly, the public grade schools did not integrate until after World War II, or about the same time Jackie Robinson signed his groundbreaking contract with the Brooklyn Dodgers. The local high school had been traditionally integrated throughout the 20th century. The high school posed as the abiding social center for inter-cultural activities.

During the post-WWII America period when Eisenhower was president and the Soviet Union was a menacing Cold War adversary; America filled in land around its cities with crafted suburbs and new home growth. Sturdily built American cars rested impatiently on cement driveways or within two-car garages.

Cars, as a transportation means, realized an upgraded role in American lifestyle in work and play. They had overcome the precept of being a novelty for the rich, and became nationally mobilized. America was in a phase of economic expansion and full employment. The Interstate Highway system allowed the garaged cars to key-up and travel more rapidly and more safely for longer distances. A decade removed from the Second World War, and virtually hours removed from fighting in Korea, Americans sought a less threatening and more frivolous existence. Train and bus excursions to Cape May continued as a valued part of the normal regional ambition. To some degree, almost every local resident benefited from Cape May's post-war vacationland popularity.

In the early fifties, green gardens and truck patches of homegrown fruits and vegetables were not a random detection in Cape May. Those practical entities helped put "garden" in the Garden State. Other portions of New Jersey became layers of suburban sandwich filling between the prodigious terminals of New York City and Philadelphia. Plow horses, poultry coops, and outhouses were vestiges of a more agrarian, and less mechanized pre-war life. Telephones had "party-lines" where a prying neighbor could listen in on other people's phone chatter. For almost a quarter of a century, first class postage stamps rested at three cents.

Cape May, consistently victimized by ravenous tidal flooding, witnessed its vaunted convention hall and popular boardwalk wash away. Although it had been an agent for splinters in the barefooted visitors, the boardwalk projected a time-honored image of durability, consistency, and family. Whether the tides were raging, or presented an East Coast Sea of Tranquility, the boardwalk framed the commercial essence of the community. It was rapidly replaced with a concrete based, asphalt-topped walkway, a fortified seawall, the Promenade.

Topographically, Cape May was either a peninsula or a cape, but in no way was it an island. It had the ocean and a bay on three of its sides. Somewhere in its history, the narrow creek that ran through must have been given a designation as a "body of water," and the area called itself "Cape Island." One cannot be a cape and an island at the same time. That is like three quarters of an oxymoron. In the competitive world of seashore resorts, descriptive hyperbole had never been in short supply, and somebody came up with its contradictory appellation.

Most of the other resort towns opted to repair their damaged wooden board walks. Cape May needed to customize its shaken image and that became, in part, the seawall. The nondescript monolith transformed into a multihued oasis of art displays and far-ranging handicraft exhibits on summer weekends, with the ever-present Atlantic as backdrop. The boardwalk's destruction was hard-felt for only a brief time, as the Promenade was born.

Full moons and low barometric pressure are a bad combination for coastal areas. The defining March 1962 nor'easter storm raised incredibly high tides. Waves crashed a mile inland, inundating homes and yards. It revealed how ill-prepared Cape May was to handle furiously foul weather. Flooding and property destruction finished off some of the resort areas along the Atlantic coast. Many towns had to reevaluate their existence and determine how to coexist with their most valuable asset, and their most imposing nemesis, the ocean. Cape May built its seawall to keep the ocean out of the city, but it could not guarantee retaining the valued sand.

Erosion of the white coastal sand had a crippling economic influence in Cape May, for without the sand there could be no beach. Many suspected with a tongue-in-cheek that the devastating '62 storm which re-mapped the coastline, was a conspiracy concocted by neighboring Wildwood. Wildwood's shoreline became massive expanses of ocean-cleansed sand. In Cape May, high tides would meet the newly constructed seawall, smothering its sand, and chasing away vacationers with unspent money clenched in their purses.

From the end of World War II through Cape May's redevelopment, African-Americans gradually supplanted first and second generation Italian-American families in their neighborhood. At first they lived side by side; then the Italians eagerly moved from the neighborhood. The Italian-Americans lost the accents of their mother tongue and utilized the whiteness of their skin to move into the WASPish community, closer to the beach, and further from the blacks. It was an unchecked ocean that started the community's change. Cape May's black section finally got caught in a revisionist undertow, and was swept up and washed away in an ensuing swirl of "urban renewal."

Blacks had about a two-decade proliferation of post-war prosperity and consequent business endeavors. Black owned bars, hotels and rooming houses, dry cleaners, barber shops and hair dressers, beach concessions, and insurance men who came to the door to collect premiums, contributed to Cape May's overall commercial presence.

Theology extended racially on parallel planes. Churches professing the same denomination sat moments from each other by walking. There was the white Baptist church; there was the black Baptist church. There was the white Methodist church; there was the black Methodist church. It was as if God needed His message translated into the same language through two cultural tongues. The root for such distinctions was seeded when Cape May imported and utilized African slaves long before the country was even chartered. Some regretful traditions die slowly.

After the schools integrated in 1947, black teachers were summarily working with white teachers. For the mainstream hotels, cooks and housekeepers remained in demand, and landscapers continued to keep the lawns manicured. For the more adventurous, work was available on commercial fishing boats that trawled the abundant ocean. Manual labor and domestic service were the recognized cornerstones of the black economy. Cape May presented a general closeness culled by its small stature and interdependent reliance on relative services. Physicians made house calls. There was home delivery by the milkman, bread man, fish man, iceman, the dry cleaner, and huckster wagons promoting fresh locally grown produce that motored down the streets. Along the way, these vendors contributed anticipated bits of news and gossip and the consequent social and cultural building blocks for a community.

Little kids, black and white, oblivious to danger, would chase the mosquito truck around the neighborhoods as part of their summertime euphoria. On foot or astride bicycles, these children were mesmerized with the billowing heavy white smoke intended to eradicate the unending wrath of the bloodsucking insects, which were multiplying in the surrounding wetlands. The kids could not rationalize that if smoke could kill mosquitoes by the droves, that it was probably not a breath of fresh air to them. So what? Smoking was a grand part of the fifties' social rituals. Un-filtered cigarettes were featured by heroes in the movies and popular publications, and vigorously chain-smoked by parents in the home. Those kids tailing the mosquito truck could not wait to be old enough to light up their own. There were other health concerns that were even more imposing.

Infantile paralysis, polio, was the pre-eminent health scourge of the day. Dreadful imagery of youngsters held captive in iron lungs supported the depth of its incredible crippling fury. The mid-fifties saw the March of Dimes campaign come forth, and with it the introduction of the Salk vaccine. Not every kid on Cape Island escaped the torment of polio. Race provided no umbrellas for exemption to this previously incurable disease. School children walked house-to-house, knocking on doors, soliciting shiny dimes and filling slotted cards with them. As much as this went to cure polio, it also provided a medium for Cape May school kids to fully work together for the first time since the elementary schools integrated.

However in many of the months, including March, black and white boys played ball in the schoolyards or went off together to catch crabs in the marshes. Somehow when they got to a certain age, they drifted apart in social circles. This was the unspoken emphasis of their upbringing. They could enjoy each other as kids, but would branch off in opposite directions when it became time to grow up.

Relationships between white and black girls were even less entwined. Girls had fewer common-based activities than the boys did, such as Little League and organized scouting events. Girls stayed closer to home. Their social sphere revolved around children of their parents' friends or girls in their neighborhood. Overall, whites made their place in Cape May, and the blacks knew theirs. Skin color was easily a contributing factor as to who went where in Cape May.

Chapter Three
The "Other" Cape May

The inveterate local weekly newspaper reported Cape May social events after World War II, touting visitations of white out-of-town relatives, young people's birthday parties, and other equally mundane happenings. The highlight of black community exploits in the paper, were miscreant deeds generally executed under the influence of alcohol. Obituaries in that paper identified the passing of black citizenry with a parenthetic notation of "colored." This was the *nom de jour* for African-Americans in Cape May and the rest of America in the forties and fifties.

The homes in the black neighborhoods were neither identified with European queens nor any other regency. The gingerbread houses with lawn parties, the vacation playgrounds for the well-heeled, were not where the black people lived. They worked for the people who had the money. Somehow they escaped the eviction notice to the developing black town, eight miles away. Many of their homes were solidly built in the early 20th century, but by the mid-fifties had fallen into a common pattern of disrepair. They were far enough removed from the vacation homes as not to violate any historical or commercial integrity. These houses were not projected on the backside of the popular two-penny picture postcards. These neighborhoods did not get a featured section in the weekly newspaper. Usually, the degenerating nature of said houses was more a reflection of the limited incomes of the proprietors than it was to endemic indifference and neglect. This was the "other Cape May."

This Cape May did not make the Chamber of Commerce brochures. The fact that these homes were no more than a ten-minute walk to the beach made the properties increasingly more valuable. As Cape May honed its image, it was quickly exhausting its buildable land. The houses around Joe's Tap took on a new seductive aura.

Seeking a better life, Puerto Ricans came to the America looking to improve their situation. Puerto Ricans were citizens of the United States, thus guaranteeing mobility to the mainland. Jobs are the key element in the survival of any people, and Puerto Ricans scrambled to find work. This expanding workforce craved unskilled, non-union labor jobs, which put them on a collision course with European immigrants, and blacks still ridding the shackles of slavery and its lingering social stigma and ramifications. Some found full-time employment on farms, while others toiled the fields during berry picking time. Some of the more robust men took jobs on fishing craft making runs into the treacherous Atlantic. Boats would frequent various harbors to unload their catches. Cape May was one such harbor.

In Cape May, blacks historically lived within two blocks on either side of the railroad tracks that entered the heart of the town, back to the small creek. Island Creek was bounded on either side by a landfill, and rimmed the black section. In geographic sequence, there was the creek, the dump, black people's homes, white family homes, and the beachfront, with property value rising, closer to the ocean.

The dump was a haven for prospecting scavengers, human and otherwise. The many trash haulers, the majority of which were black, would unload their trucks, and people would go to the dump to sift through the refuse for a hidden treasure. Many fires were lit to eliminate the mounting trash. Full sized rats flourished and contentedly made their homes there, with a few forays into nearby homes in cold weather. Marauding sea gulls flocked to the dump for festive family meals.

A bumpy unpaved gravel road crossed a rickety wooden bridge that merged the boundary of the communities Cape May and West

Cape May, with the creek resting beneath, rising and waning with the prevailing tides. Trash and junk were unwittingly and repeatedly discarded over the railing of the small bridge. What could have been a wonderful natural resource amid the scenic meadow, marshlands, and the winding creek, found the dump as the embodiment of a festering health hazard and eyesore. The low tide exposed the junk, resting in an incongruous stench-laden serenity. This impression was not lost on the image-conscious people of Cape May.

At the western end of the train station, across Lafayette Street was Joe's Tap. Joe's Tap had a sturdy red brick exterior with a simple ninety-degree angled, 1920s style architecture, and stood three stories high. Italian-Americans Giuseppe, or "Joe," and Mary Di Cicco owned it. Joe's Tap merged the transition of African-American expansion into existing Italian-American culture that had blossomed in the town from the earliest days of the 20th century.

The jukebox perpetually thumped the rhythmic heartbeat of Joe's Tap. The black discs that had the big hole in the center, 45 rpm, energized the customers. Lloyd Price, Fats Domino, and Dinah Washington music moved through the smoky air as patrons talked louder and louder to be heard over it. Feet bounced and tapped, and fingers snapped. Music would inspire dancing; dancing would encourage thirst. Behind the bar, two jars of pickled pig's feet sat near a jar of boiled eggs, and a jar of large pickles, as the snacks of choice. A couple of racks of pretzels and potato chips, in small cellophane bags, balanced the culinary delicacies that might influence additional thirst. The fifties were a time when men occasionally wore dress hats and ties while engaging in social events.

During the week, or in the slow winter months, Joe's Tap relied on package goods sales and loyal local regulars to keep a healthy flow of business. The mirrored wall behind the bar braced shelves filled with colorful bottles of various liquors and spirits. A couple of well-worn green felted pool tables witnessed dollar bills change hands from friendly wagering. There were twelve small tables on the black and white checker-tiled floor, each seemingly weighed down by ashtrays in usual need of being emptied, surrounded by bar chairs.

A cigarette machine sat nearby to offer assurance that the ashtrays remained filled. Saturday night was a big deal, as mostly black people would reacquaint with friends or maybe indulge someone they met earlier on the beach. More than one illicit rendezvous blossomed from Joe's Tap.

Joe was a small guy, with a neatly trimmed mustache, who had serious ideas about garnering a piece of the American dream. His family left Sicily following WWI. Joe and Mary married the June before the bombing of Pearl Harbor. At age thirty, he enlisted in the Army in 1942 as a down payment towards securing his dream. His unit fought near Palermo, Sicily that was the hometown of his now-migrated parents, and place of his birth. He got to see much of the old country while in the service, and had as much fun as he could have within the context of a war. He also saw action in northern Africa, and France. He survived the D-Day invasion in 1944. Mary served the war effort as a volunteer in a military rehabilitation hospital, converted from a local hotel.

As soldiers returned from the war, Joe sought to further fulfill his dreams. Upon his discharge in late 1945, he and Mary purchased the bar, Mary and her side of the family fronted the bulk of the funding. Joe ran the bar and the physical part of the operation. Mary, who cut a dynamic figure in her younger days, was progressively expanding into an untidy large woman. Mary managed the business end of Joe's Tap. She paid the bills, did the banking, and affected most of the employee related details. She had her own serious ideas of what the American dream was. Both of their parents entered America through the immigration portal of Ellis Island and eventually settled locally; her family just before the First World War, and his in 1922. The placement of the bar was absolute ground zero, geographically, for an emerging black community trying to assert its own viability during a time of national racial consciousness. Their bar did well and became the epicenter of black social activity and drinking.

Joe and Mary would hire bartenders and other help as needed. Riding a wave of up-tempo post-war growth, bar help would come and go as opportunities became available elsewhere. Their only regular employee lived on the premises upstairs. Mo Finch was a bartender at night and sub-contracted out heavy earth-moving equipment during the day. The backyard of Joe's Tap formerly had an outhouse, and currently housed a parked bulldozer, a front-end loader, a mud-laden dump truck, and usually about a dozen caged, cackling, laying hens, and a rooster protected by the ferocious looking collie, Benito. Benito was never leashed, and drunks and prowlers did not breach the fence for a free egg.

Mo Finch was a handsome, hard-working, black man in his thirties, who was also the Joe's Tap handyman. Mo still had not invested the requisite time to grow up. He was in the Army during WWII and got married to a high school girl, not long after his discharge. Mo was nine years his bride's senior.

Mo was born in Cape May, and raised as a Baptist. He could be articulately sophisticated or wantonly vulgar and surly, depending upon whom he was trying to make an impact. Both Joe and Mary duly noted his appeal for different reasons. Joe liked Mo's ability to impart his charm on the bar patrons and induce the regulars and visitors alike to return again and again. It was Mo's affable vibe that permeated the bar. Mo could be trusted around the money and was readily available in a pinch. Plus, Mo could fix anything, and save the bar money on repairs. Joe had no problem with Mo. Together, they made the bar a desired place to pass the time. They were friends.

Mo, incorrigibly, saw life through a wandering eye after his marriage. The birth of a daughter in 1949 did little to settle his instincts. By 1950, he separated from his wife and moved with his infant daughter to work and live at Joe's Tap. His defection from the marriage was not that surprising. However, taking the baby was puzzling and caused the mother periods of debilitating desperation.

Mary was attracted to Mo. No, Mary was *attracted* to Mo! Mary and Mo were not so secret lovers. As integrated association moved into the American scheme with a more urgent calling for the military, professional sports, and public education, interracial romance was not. Mary and Mo were social pioneers of sorts.

In the early days of television, religious ministries were represented by Billy Graham, Oral Roberts, and Bishop Fulton J. Sheen. Televangelism helped guide the moral formation of post-war religion in America. It shaped the template for spiritual and ethical living.

Creating their own moral code, Mary and Mo were living an adulterous life at Joe's Tap. This was an awkward but workable situation. Everyone in the bar knew of Mary's affinity for Mo, and Mo was not shy about saying as much. It was also thought that Mary furtively instigated Mo's estrangement from his wife and helped Mo gain custody of the baby. She immediately moved them into the bar. The fact that a fiscally tight-fisted Mary co-signed the financing of Mo's trucks and business ventures and provided for him a place to live was the overriding quintessence of Mo's attraction to her. He would never gnaw on the hand that fed him, but he was not beyond taking a naughty outside nibble from time to time when temptation presented itself.

In 1952, Mo's divorce was granted and so were permanent and exclusive custodial rights to his daughter. The original notice for the final custody hearing was scheduled for one o'clock on a Wednesday, and Mo's ex-wife, Helena, was completely prepared. She and her family exhorted character witnesses and letters of reference from clergy, teachers, employers, and friends. Mysteriously, she did not receive a subsequent notice that the hearing was reset for nine that same morning. She was never able to present her witnesses and supporting evidence.

Mary marshaled Mo and the baby away in a car as Helena, escorted by her parents, walked determinedly toward the courthouse. Mo never looked back.

Helena ingested a bottle of anti-depressant sleeping pills following the ruling. She had been married, bore a child, got divorced, lost custody, became depressed, and tried to relieve her anguish and shame in a legitimate suicide attempt, all before her twenty-second birthday. She survived the pills, but did not recover from the sordidness of all this until the 1960s, following the birth of her second child in 1959, and a series of institutionalized therapies.

She would have a couple more children after that. She remarried only after her fourth child.

Mary posed as a controlling guru, while Mo adjusted his life. As Helena moved back with her parents in New York, Mo became legally and logistically detached from her, and at Mary's urging, eliminated any chance for her to craft a practical relationship with their daughter. In an effort to restore her own inner peace and sanity, Helena removed herself from any residual emotional attachment and accompanying memory of her life with Mo and, by extension, the birth of her first child. She achieved this through chronic internal turmoil and countless hours of clinical supervision. Years, many years, finally allowed her to erase this despondent decade from her life. She came to accept life without either Mo or the child. She struggled with the magnitude of her plight, yet she allowed for her cognizance of the past to mercifully dissipate, and found stability in rearing her children.

Chapter Four *Little Mo*

M o lived in an apartment on the second floor of Joe's Tap with his daughter, Maurine, or "Little Mo" as she was dubbed. The unique spelling of Maurine's name was a tribute her father, Maurice, had bestowed upon himself. This was the only home Little Mo knew. Also on that floor were Mary's sister Carmen and her two children, Antonio and Ella. As time went on, they all co-existed as a not-so-happy family, or at least as happy as they could be in a bar rife with inherent dysfunction.

When Mo was not trying to impress Mary, he found time to have fun and laugh with his daughter on occasion. When Maurine was two, Mo took her to see Santa Claus come to town. Santa showed up as promised, all decked out in a surplus Korean War helicopter, painted red and green for the occasion. In front of hundreds of anxious kids and parents, the helicopter had a problem with the wind and crashed on the beach sand. Little Mo giggled at all the commotion. Fortunately no one got hurt. Maurine did not know anything about Santa Claus, but she enjoyed being with her dad. She thought her dad staged all of that for her. This particular yuletide experience provided the most eventful Christmas Maurine would see for a couple decades.

Joe and Mary had a larger apartment on the second floor, but they rarely shared it. There was a maze of seldom used sleeping rooms and a storage area on the third floor. At one time the sleeping rooms were rented out by the hour for the carnal convenience of the fishermen. However, Joe and Mary recognized that this arrangement was the source for much of the conflict that found its way to the bar.

Following a raucous bar battle, Joe banned customers from going up the steps for any reason; thus discontinued the informal hourly rental of the rooms. Without any other useful intent looming, the third floor promptly became a repository for dust, and a graveyard for bar junk.

For kindergarten, Little Mo matriculated in the public school. Ella, who was the same age as Little Mo and born into a Catholic family, went to public school with her. There was no kindergarten at the Catholic school. They were in a totally integrated environment with black and white classmates. Most of the kids had *two* parents, which caused Little Mo to seek answers to her puzzlement as to why she did not have a mother. Little Mo seemingly inherited her father's charm and wit; however, she picked her spots to find happiness and show her true personality. She was having a full-blown identity crisis that no one around her would remedy. Her living situation also created a clouded image of what race her mother was (her mother was a darker-skinned Puerto Rican).

The train depot sat across the street from Joe's Tap. On occasion, Little Mo would leave the side porch of the bar, cross the busy street, and wait for the late afternoon train. She would wistfully ask disembarking women, usually black women, "Are you my Mommy?" The daily commuters would try to look away as Little Mo would query would-be mothers. This was a difficult question to figure out the basis for, and "No, I am not!" certainly could not posture as an adequate retort, however its accuracy. For her, this was a legitimate question, as she had no contact with her real mother. Little Mo could not understand why that was, but she knew her mother could possibly be on the next train. The only images of her mother were the ones projected in her dreams. The faces she saw in those dreams included at different times, gospel singer Mahalia Jackson, entertainer Pearl Bailey and First Lady Mamie Eisenhower. She surely did not want to miss her whoever she was. Mo did nothing to accommodate his daughter's investigation and Little Mo was stranded with far more questions than answers.

Little Mo would have to prepare for school with only Ella in attendance. They would have to find their own breakfast. When available, they would grab a boiled egg from the bar's outdated icebox. The combing and braiding of a black girl's hair is work for even the most ardent of mothers. To be five-years-old and having to comb one's own hair, with only five-year-old Ella for assistance, was impossible. Little Mo did her own hair.

Once during the school year, a female customer of Joe's, recognizing this wretched shortcoming, combed Little Mo's hair. Following this time-consuming consideration, she offered to straighten Little Mo's hair later in the week. The woman, Bertha Fowler, was a regular in the bar. Mo and Mary met her offer with resounding indifference. Little Mo lobbied with tearful perseverance to allow for the project to take place, and so it did. The resulting rehab in Little Mo's look was remarkable. She felt much better about herself. She proceeded to ask her father for the supplies to fix her hair, herself. It took him more than a month to get them, but he complied. Her Christmas presents in kindergarten were a curling iron, hot comb, and a jar of pomade. That was her entire gift repertoire. Little Mo would not again have her hair done by anyone other than herself, until eighth grade.

Starting in first grade, Little Mo, at Mary's insistence, began going to the Catholic grade school along with Ella. Now moving into the fourth grade, Little Mo had faced racial invectives and insults almost on a daily basis at school. In school, each day was a public execution. Little Mo was the first and only black person at that school, in any capacity, during her time there. Little Mo's nicknames during her early years included "Brillo-head," "Eggplant" and "Little Slow." The latter had to do with Little Mo's way of walking and a play on her name. She was never in a hurry to get to school or hustle on the playground.

Little Mo would don her dark tartan blue uniform and go to school. The public school kids would pass her by, going to their school. She saw the kids she had been in class with while in kindergarten. Most of those kids she remembered and liked, and with whom she wanted to associate. For a girl on the chubby side, who wore glasses, had marginally combed hair, had a mole on her chin, and had but one real friend in the school in Ella, life could not have been worse. Neither Little Mo nor Ella got invitations to visit their classmates' homes. Certainly none were extended for kids to come to a bar.

The snide remarks by the nuns and the more open comments by the kids happened around the same time as the *Brown v Board of Education* Supreme Court ruling. This decision allowed for an equal education for any American child. Schools were not allowed to be separate and equal based on race. The Montgomery, Alabama bus boycott established that Americans were not predisposed to sit in assigned sections of public transportation. This case made public figures of Rosa Parks and a young preacher named Martin Luther King. The integration of Little Rock, Arkansas's Central High School became a federal case when black students were barred from entering the school for their education. At the time, it was the biggest challenge to the *Brown* decision. The launching of the Soviet *Sputnik* made Americans aware that the Soviets were a capable and imposing foe. These events peppered Little Mo's early school years.

Skeptical classmates related to events in the news and on television that their parents feared and commented on--communism and black people. Consensus was that Little Mo was probably not a commie, but she sure as hell was black. Little Mo's ebullience lay hidden behind a defensive scowl. She was a living, tangible symbol of the things that alarmed the white kids' parents of that era. She said very little, but was subjected to harangues as if she was invisible.

Little Mo and Ella fed the chickens and harvested the eggs. This proved to be a chore they tolerated. The girls found the penning of the poultry did not seem quite fair. They were continually reminded of their own situation. They soon learned that it was not good practice to adopt one of the hens as a pet. As they got comfortable with a favorite chicken, Mo would kill it for a Sunday meal and they would eat it. For both girls, this was just added to their childhood dis-illusions.

One of the more rewarding tasks Little Mo had occasion to enjoy was when the jukebox man, Elmo, would come to the bar and she would "help" him. Elmo was a German Jewish immigrant who spent the final three years of World War II miraculously clinging to life in the horrid confines of the Nazi concentration camp in Auschwitz, Poland. Elmo, who was in his mid-thirties, would come every couple of weeks to collect the money and change the records in the jukebox. Conversation with Elmo was different from what the other adults offered. He told Little Mo stories and jokes. In the early days, neither of their English was very advanced, but their vocabularies seemed to move forward at about the same speed. Little Mo waded through Elmo's broken English. He found enjoyment in her youthful interest. Somehow they connected to each other's dispositions. They kept each other company while Elmo serviced the machines.

As a teenager, Elmo saw his parents and older brother killed in the camp. Elmo had inexplicably escaped death from exposure, illness, and malnutrition. His life was spared only when the Russians liberated the camp at the end of the war. He weighed seventy-nine pounds when the camp was freed at age nineteen.

Elmo was rejuvenated by the Red Cross and made his way to Cherry Hill, New Jersey, by way of Canada. People in his synagogue tutored him to improve his English. At the same time, he studied to be an electrician. He worked his way through trade school by servicing juke boxes. In a short time, Elmo started his vending machine company. He had other employees and was on the road less and less, but he enjoyed coming to Cape May as part of his routine. One hot summer day while Elmo was tending to his job, a seven-year-old Little Mo asked, "Why do you have that number on your arm?" She was captivated by the tattooed link to his days of depraved consignment in Auschwitz.

"It helps me remember my family: my mother, father, and brother." Elmo tried to explain the ghastly numbers in terms that Little Mo might comprehend.

"Oh Mister Elmo, I want to get my own number, so I can remember my mother!"

"Little Mo, I am sorry, but they ran out of these kinds of numbers at the end of the big war." Elmo's thick German accent was a dominant factor in his English. Little Mo stuck with it hoping to find out more about the purpose of the number on his arm.

"Well I wish I had something to remember my mother, and I guess it doesn't have to be a number!" Little Mo was dejected, but thrived on the interaction with Elmo, and searched for a sense of maternal association.

Elmo scratched his head, and said, "I'll tell you what Little Mo, you can have these records. When you play them, it might help you get closer to your mother. I hope someday that you'll see your mother. I won't have the chance to see mine."

Every time Elmo visited to work on the jukebox, he would give Little Mo a few of the records that were scratched or outdated. For Little Mo, their condition did not matter, somebody had given her something; something that meant hope, and that she could use forever. Little Mo did not have a record player, but saved the records and thought of Elmo and her non-existent mother as they mounted over the years. The talks with Elmo were like well-timed vacations for Little Mo. It was evident to Elmo how bright Little Mo was and how much she was missing. He appreciated her innocence and spirit.

Little Mo would go into the isolated attic, where she stored her growing record collection, and share her fun and good fortune with Ella. They would not play the records for they had no record player. However, as Little Mo sorted through them, the girls would sing the songs that they had heard in the jukebox or on the radio. The attic was their "hideaway." It was their tree house without limbs. It was a retreat that insulated them from Mary; a lair of refuge she would customarily not intrude. Even in the winter months when the attic had little heat climbing up the steps from the second floor, they would get together and sing. They clapped to tunes with mittens on their hands while their breath took shape in the form of a cold, white, vapor, which rapidly disappeared amid a network of cobwebs and dust.

During the summer months, the girls would do the same thing they did in the winter, except they would both work up a pouring sweat as the attic had little ventilation and the screens in the windows did little to bring a soothing breeze into the room.

Approaching age eleven, Little Mo was getting taller and losing the puffy baby-fat that caused so much consternation in her early days in school. She still wore the uniform to school and had the glasses, but she was aware of personal changes taking place, inevitable female changes. One thing Little Mo learned a long time ago was that Mary was not going to help. Most of her education about life as a budding young woman came from paying attention to what the female customers talked about.

Little Mo was in charge of certain things in her life that had not been afforded to her before. The time in the attic, and property in the form of records that she could call her own, gave her space and purpose. At the time Cape May was sliding into the 1960s and going through an unsolicited makeover of its own, Little Mo took a big step and insisted on being called, "Maurine."

Chapter Five *Business Woman*

Mo had no reservations about discussing his relationship concerning Mary with people in the bar, but sought to keep that removed from Maurine. Despite his consideration for her, Mo was not all that discrete. More than once Maurine had walked in on Mo and Mary while they were involved in romantic activity. When she was younger she was not moved by it, and just thought they were taking a frenetic nap. As she got older, she not only realized that Mo and Mary were together, but together all the time. She also realized that Joe had to know about this as well. Yet worse than all of this, was that Mary tried to act like a mother to her, without the salient passion or interest of a mother. Her austere authoritarian, demeanor unsettled Maurine. Mo was her father, but he was oddly hypnotized by the portly Mary. Mo offered only sporadic encouragement or support for Maurine to expand. Joe went with the flow. He knew that Mo and Mary were an item under his roof, but he needed both of them for business reasons. He was also at a stage in his life when he was losing his eyesight and the will to singularly combat such a menacing deficit.

Maurine and Ella sat on the side porch of the bar, which doubled as their home. They watched cars and people amble by. They formed an Ebony and Ivory version of the sixties. The siren of the daily noon alarm would screech from the fire station a block away. Benito snuggled peacefully at their feet. When the siren rang out, Benito would lift his head and howl along with it. This was their life. Not many kids grow up in a bar.

During the early sixties a number of events came forth to make an impression on the girls and the community. The local public high school moved from its traditional spot in downtown Cape May to a cornfield in an adjoining township. Now all of the students were required to board a yellow school bus for high school. As the new school settled and began to develop a more rural identity than the previous high school, the shiny new buses created an opportunity for the students from the homes in the area that was the Other Cape May to unite on the same bus. They noted how many of the riders were black. In short order they adopted a new name for their amber chariot. They christened their transport with the rhyming name as "Bus 13--the African Queen." The boardwalk and convention hall became a pile of rubble following the March 1962 storm. The town now had no high school, no boardwalk, no convention hall and a cluster of memories that were tied to those now-vanished cultural entities. Cape May stumbled through a brief period in search of its new identity. Plans were also underway to launch a ferry service across the Delaware Bay and link up with its neighbors from the First State. The ferry would provide a new source of transport to the resort.

During this period, the city decided to move the depot a block shorter than where it had been, and redo the station area with retail shops. The train did not cross Lafayette Street. This kept traffic moving, and was not bogged down by the flashing red railroad lights and the flexing barrier that had been the anticipated norm for so many years, when the train entered or departed. Now the station was right next door to Joe's Tap. The elimination of the pillared columns supporting its peaked overhang was the prelude to more extensive modifications the area around Joe's Tap would soon be encountering.

The dump which had been the source of so much civic second-guessing also relocated. It was moved to a more secluded area in an adjacent community. The eyesore, smell, and rodents were banished from the area. The escalating fiscal potential of the perimeter properties magnified. The junk was removed from the creek; seagulls sought new haunts.

These re-shuffled entities did not affect anything at Joe's Tap. Mary still made both girls work in and around the bar. They filled the cigarette machine, polished the furniture, tended the chickens, and made up the rooms upstairs. They did it literally for no money. They were slaves without the title. The more they did, the more Mary demanded. As they got older, the more frustrated they became with their aimless and unappreciated situation. Maurine was more likely to vocalize such sentiments, but there were no practical options. Ella would burst into tears. Male customers also began noticing the undeniable growth of both girls.

Ella and Maurine were each other's best friends. Five months apart in age, the girls had done so many things together, from sharing problems to physically protecting each other against mosquitoes or insensitive name calling in school. They harmonized to records that made no sound. Maurine's issues were more easily read, and showed the strength and perseverance to endure them. Ella made a point to stay close to Maurine.

Ella was neither as sharp intellectually, nor was she emerging with the female form that Maurine was. Ella was quiet but more reactive emotionally. She was overweight, and riddled with crying spells, fueled by seemingly little provocation. Although she lived with her mother and brother, Ella wanted and probably needed more attention than she got. Her mother Carmen's relationship with her father dissolved before anything more substantial than an unwanted pregnancy could ever develop. He never returned when he found out about his impending paternity. Carmen failed to get over this slight and showered much of the blame on Ella. The fact that he had a wife and three children in New York may have played a part in his disappearing from Joe's Tap and Carmen's life. Ella's father was a light-skinned Puerto Rican fisherman who came to Cape May on a series of stopovers. His skin-tone allowed Ella to sustain her Iberian genetic identity without much inquest by her classmates. Ella looked eerily like Carmen, only with curlier black hair. Carmen looked very much like Mary, but was a couple years older and had a trimmer figure. Carmen surely had a less settled constitution.

Carmen was not opposed to a good time. It was not a rare happenstance that she would be missing in action from home for days at a time. Carmen's maternal influence with her children in Cape May was no more involved than it was with her older kids. She had two boys who lived with their paternal grandparents in Detroit. Ella only knew of those brothers from old black and white photos. The older boys were born during the war, with the second brother born fifteen months *after* Carmen's husband had been fighting in the Pacific. Carmen's marriage ended in divorce shortly after her husband's discharge, and he gained custody of *both* children.

Carmen's father-in-law was an influential figure in the community who had developed an extensive underworld resume, which helped wrest custody from Carmen. Carmen's ex-husband was eventually killed in a gangland shootout in the streets of Detroit, an occupational hazard of his family's businesses. Her former in-laws assumed full responsibility in raising the boys. This was a position that they had already played in large part, prior to the death of Carmen's ex-husband. Carmen maintained cursory contact, but did not occupy an integral part in their lives. Her vindictive and connected in-laws saw to that.

Ella's brother, older than her by three years, Antonio, was full of mischief bordering on juvenile delinquency. Antonio lived his young life like he was an airplane missing an aileron. He had a fun-loving personality, but had no restraints on his heading. He had a different father from Ella and did not have any idea who that was. He was put out of parochial school after the first grade. He *had* to go to the public school, and for his troubles, got to repeat first grade. Ella had little in common with Antonio; his hair was a more brownish, and he was lighter in skin tone. Antonio was less shackled to the bar. He had considerably more leeway in carousing the streets and beaches. There was more than subtle resentment toward Ella by her mother and aunt, which Ella failed to understand. There were times that Ella and Antonio thought that things could be better for both of them. But whom could they tell? Carmen? Mary? Joe? Both of them comfortably confided in a youthful, but discerning, Maurine.

The fun times did not happen often, and for Maurine, those times happened much easier when Mary was not around. However, a couple times Mo took Mary and the kids to a drive-in movie theater. The cartoons preceding the feature were worth the drive. Yet the content of the motion picture would soon be diminished, first, by a wave of voracious mosquitoes entering the open windows of Mary's car, and then by inevitable drowsiness and slumber, which intruded soon after the main feature began.

One summer evening a year, Mo would take the kids to the Wildwood boardwalk for its myriad of amusement rides and frozen custard stands. When she was younger, this was fun for Maurine. Being out with her father and thrilled by the rides, and walking among thousands of people seeking a good time, held more allure for her when she was seven and eight than when she neared thirteen. Her father did not see his little girl growing up, and she was almost as tall as he was. Maurine's grasp of herself and life around her was forming a more structured outline. Her vision of what she wanted from life was becoming far more involved than a stroll on a boardwalk, or falling asleep at the drive-in. As her grade school years were winding down, Maurine did not view herself as a kid, but was not sure how to shake that outdated image.

Maurine paid attention to the people in the bar and observed things they talked about. Maybe she was trying to find an enlightened path to her teenage years. She also watched what they drank. Over the years, she could not understand the changes that people went through when they drank alcohol. Some of them changed in a dramatic way. They repeatedly paid money to go through those changes. There were times when she thought they were funny, and other times their surly condition brought pity or fear. Living in a bar acquainted her with drinks and drunkenness in a first-hand way.

By the time she was twelve, Maurine had taken the effort to explore many of the offerings of Joe's Tap. Most of those experimental sips were done out of view of Mary or Mo. She vowed that alcohol was not imprinted on the lifestyle of her future. Although she did not remember a particular reaction, except for a couple of times she woke up in the morning and could not recall how she got to bed.

She found the taste of most of her exploits repulsive. However, in the end, she noted that the bar patrons habitually paid for their drinks and the peculiar way they behaved.

By her teenage years, even though she wore the uniform to school, Maurine wanted money for clothing and incidentals that other girls her age sought. Maurine and Mo had more than one inane discussion about an allowance. At the end of such a session he would reach into his pocket and hand Maurine some loose change. Maurine confronted Mary in more than one discussion about getting a decent wage from working in the bar. Mary acceded to give her a "salary" that did not come close to being a minimum hourly wage. Maurine came to loathe Mary for a number of things and would stand up to Mary more as time went on.

As Maurine entered the eighth grade her baby-fat had totally gone away. She was five-feet-nine with a woman's body that the Catholic school uniform could not easily mask. The men in the bar were approaching her, with caution, but came on to her just the same. Having Mo and Mary there was an indelible, personified deterrent to anything beyond work for Maurine, or a half-buzzed lecher lurking for a delectable conquest.

For Maurine, battles with her father about money became miserable footnotes in an overall unhappy adolescence. He would chide her by saying, "Why can't you be more like Ella?" His meaning was to "know your place and shut up!" Maurine desired things of substance, and not just be known as the "girl who lives in the bar." From about the fifth grade, the kids teased and goaded Maurine about getting them beer or liquor. One day after such prodding, and feeling the sting of her latest blow-up with Mary, Maurine decided to fill an "order" for some of her classmates. She authored ground-rules for a liquor sale and crafted counter measures against being exposed. She would take orders on Thursday and deliver on Friday; cash only, no credit.

On Friday morning, when the rooster crowed at first light, before the adults got up, she would go into the bar and claim the necessary stock. She packed a spare school bag and hid it behind the wheels of a nearby railroad car that had been converted into a theme restaurant. She retrieved it after school. The buyers would meet her behind the American Legion building, across the street from the school, five minutes after the last class on Friday. The building had no activity during the day and had large hedges to provide cover. She commanded her customers to have a book bag or gym bag large enough not to bring attention to its contents. She also restricted the sales to pints and fifths of hard liquor; wine was too bulky and beer was too cheap. She also set her own prices, for it was all profit. At a time when fifths were around three dollars, she sold them for five dollars. Pints went for two dollars. Since bottles of liquor were broken down into shots at the bar, an accurate accountability of the inventory was never a problem. By this time she took the inventory for the bar, anyway. She cleared almost forty dollars on the first go-round. She discovered that holidays and long weekends provided an even heftier sales binge. She now had money and the know-how to get more.

As silly and simple as this entrepreneurial endeavor was, it survived the whole school year. Her only overhead was the purchase of a couple larger book bags at the local five and ten department store. With her windfall, Maurine shopped from the Sears and Roebuck catalog. No one at home paid attention to Maurine's growing stash of clothes and accessories, or the delivered shipments in the mail. All of this far exceeded the limits of her paltry salary.

Her customers were alcoholics before they reached high school. They looked up to Maurine. It mattered not to Maurine how these kids came about the money. All of them were the products of a Catholic school education. She illuminated as the "expert" among her peers; she had gained their respect. This was a status in which Maurine reveled.

Although she yearned for entrance into the public high school, Maurine's self-esteem and appearance exploded during her freshman year in the Catholic high school. She got fitted for contact lenses. Contacts were a novelty at that time for a young person. She ordered a standing appointment each month at a licensed hairdresser. Perhaps her most pleasurable self-indulgence was the hi-fi record player she had delivered. In the solace of her room, Maurine listened to the hundreds of 45s Elmo had given her over years. Her favorite tunes were the Motown records, and smooth sounding Johnny Mathis songs. Johnny Mathis just cried out for romance. Maybe Maurine could find out about that someday. She had come a long way from being the ridiculed, pudgy, nappy haired, "colored girl with glasses," in the early years of school. Now that she was beginning to like herself, maybe a boy could too.

Chapter Six *Chris*

During the summer of 1964, Mary took steps to extend her business empire. She purchased a small corner store, a block from the bar, from an older Italian lady who moved from the neighborhood. She secured some other properties as well. The lady, who never mastered the English language, had run the store at that location since the 1930s. Her advancing age and a dwindling of constituent Italians made it an ideal time for her to retire to another part of Cape Island. The little store was on one of the only all black streets in Cape May. The store stocked candy, ice cream, pretzels and potato chips, soda pop, bread, toilet paper, and some standard canned goods. The pint-sized neighborhood convenience store was the forerunner to the modern, franchised, Seven-Eleven types. Maurine was the designated clerk. She was a couple months shy of her fifteenth birthday. She had completed her freshman year at the Catholic high school in nearby Wildwood.

Maurine's figure had filled out. Her face had a stunning model quality to it; she was pretty in any context. The mole on her chin had become a gosh-honest beauty mark. She laughed more easily than she did as a youngster. It was not so coincidental that a local athlete from the public high school made a point to pass by the store on a daily basis during the summer, coming from the nearby outdoor basketball courts. He always had enough money for an ice cream bar or certainly a penny pretzel rod. His dividend for buying the pretzel rod was Maurine's undivided attention. An investment of a couple of pennies also bought the additional bonus of teenage chat and the weaning of puppy love. Maurine was amused with Chris Mitchell's kidding, and she appreciated his pointed awareness of her.

Aside from the guys to whom she sold the booze, and they did not really count, no one else had ever pursued her because they just wanted to be around her. No one else had ever looked her in the eye, with equal allocation during a conversation, other than Mr. Elmo. Chris wanted to be around her and he wanted to talk to her. When growing up as kids, Chris had seen the round black girl on the porch of the bar, with the menacing dog looming close by, like a Secret Service agent around the president. He figured to stay away from both of them. That was then, this is now!

Chris had distinguished himself in school as a varsity football and track athlete. He was working on his basketball skills hoping to make the varsity in his junior year. He was also involved in other school projects, which made him popular among his schoolmates. Chris stood over six feet, was solidly built, and presented a timely sense of humor and a respectful set of manners. He worked at a breakfast-lunch restaurant, across the street from the beach, as a dishwasher. He had worked at the public tennis courts a few years before, but got fired for going off to play baseball when he was supposed to have dragged the clay courts, and did not. He had a newspaper route leading up to high school, but stopped that when the football season started. His younger brother, Stevie, occasionally came with him into the store, and succeeded Chris at those jobs. As sports had been his life up to now, his eye on Maurine was even more formidable.

Following a couple weeks of pretzel rod chatter, Chris asked Maurine when she could walk on the beach with him. Knowing that her time was precious, for she seemed to be in the store every time he passed, he did not expect a positive reply. "I'll meet you at the Raymond Street beach at three o'clock tomorrow," she stated without hesitation. This was a surprise response, and much to Chris's delight.

At three the next day, Chris was anxiously planted on a Promenade bench waiting for Maurine. She showed up as promised. The sun sparkled off her brown, well-oiled skin. Her eyes were hidden behind a pair of cool looking five and dime sunglasses. A white t-shirt with turquoise trim and medium length white shorts accented Maurine's shapely legs. Her straightened hair was wrapped in a white scarf with turquoise paisley markings. She had brown leather sandals on her feet.

Chris sat there in his raggedly cut-off short brown pants, and a red and yellow madras button-up shirt that he left unbuttoned, with the sleeves removed up to the shoulder. The rippling, bulging biceps he had worked on justified the alteration of the shirt. He wore high top black Chuck Taylor Converse sneakers with no socks. He had an insipid brownish baseball cap on his head. The visor of which shielded the bright glare from the imposing sun. Their clashing "style" depicted a snippet of a "beauty and the beast" component.

Bathers soaked up the brilliant sunlight. Suntanned lifeguards manned their perches in the elevated seats above the sand. The waves behaved themselves on a serene weekday. Since neither of them had done anything like this before; everything Maurine and Chris said, did, or went to, broke new ground. That summer, and particularly this day, was their introduction to real life adulthood dilemmas.

Maurine sat on the bench with Chris, and took a deep breath to savor her rare minutes of freedom. She looked longingly onto the tranquil water's edge where mothers were holding the hands of their children, going into the water or coming from it, so contentedly united.

"I am glad you showed," said Chris.

"I said three-o'clock!" She countered.

"Well I got here at two-fifteen to make sure I got a good bench." Benches up and down the walk were conspicuously vacant.

"Am I that special?" Maurine asked.

"I hope so!" Chris replied.

They both took their footwear off and walked in the warm sand. Colorful beach umbrellas, and sprawled out blankets and towels, bordered by folding beach chairs were the only impediments along their landmark stroll. They passed in front of orange canvas covered cabanas. Would-be bathers hiding from the sun, or drying off from a refreshing dip found solace in them. They trod a rock jetty of jumbo-sized boulders that were supposed to keep the sand from escaping the beach. The apathetic waves splashed near people further down the jetty. They had fishing rods aimed into the ocean and were concentrating on their next catch. The briny spray gave cooling reprieve to the anglers. Seagulls soared and squealed, while spying for an unsuspecting tourist to put a hot dog down so they could swoop off with a relished tidbit. Pleasure boats and yachts lolled on the horizon unaware of these teenagers making tracks in the sand. Neither Maurine nor Chris encouraged any more attention than what they otherwise got, which was none. They liked the solitude of their journey.

They made it to the cove at the end of the Promenade. The Cape May Point Lighthouse, which rested at the foot of the cape was straight ahead, but that was a couple miles away. Both of them had an agenda that did not include walking all the way to the lighthouse. From where they stood at the base of the cove, they could not only view the lighthouse but the red roof of the large Catholic convent where nuns would have summer retreats. There was also a weather-beaten concrete World War II bunker that was positioned such that it could halt Nazi submarines of bygone days from entering the Delaware Bay.

The conversation was sparing, but Chris did grab Maurine's hand, to her fascination, and they sauntered in the sand like lovers on-screen in the movies, or as Maurine visualized, in a Johnny Mathis song. Looking past their disparate outfits, they matched up quite well. She was tall; he was taller. He was brown; she was browner. And they both were getting darker walking into the westward moving afternoon sun.

Chris led Maurine to a sea-grass covered sand dune, out of view from any direction. In a deliberate motion, he dropped his sneakers, turned his hat backwards, pulled Maurine to him, and kissed her. She responded. They were kissing, and breathing in an unfamiliar erratic fashion. Wow! Chris coyly ran his hand up the inside of Maurine's top and gently massaged her ample breast. Her bra remained in place, and he did not think to move any more forward than that. Maurine made reasonably sure he did not go any further with this, and smacked his hand.

"Why'd you hit me?"

"Why'd you squeeze my boob?"

"I'd never felt one before!"

"Yeah, and that's exactly what it felt like. Like you didn't know what you were doing."

"Ah, the voice of experience, so are you going to let me practice and get it right?"

"Someday I will, if you act right!"

"What do I have to do, get straight A's?"

"I know you're smart, but that's not it. You'll figure it out. Plus you'd probably forge your report card!"

Chris was not sure what she meant. But at least it sounded promising.

They both understood they had to quit what they were doing pretty soon, but how soon? They laid down behind the dune and kissed and talked and giggled. Sand invaded their clothing from head to toe. They exulted in the intimacy. However, at 15 and 16 there was plenty of time left to do the things their bodies were strongly suggesting. "Did you notice those married people back there? I mean what moves people to like each other?" Chris pondered out loud.

"What are you asking?"

"Look, there were some good looking men with some eh…not so good looking women, right? And vice versa, you know!"

"So are you saying that we are a mismatch?"

"Actually, I am thinking how perfect we are!" Chris's youthful idealism may have been infected by his aroused libido.

"Perfect? Well, I don't think I am perfect, but by the time we get to be forty, neither of us will look like this. If we still know each other, ask those questions then!" As much as Maurine was enjoying her time with Chris, she did not allow herself to become overwrought with optimism. Still, there was nothing that had ever made her feel this good.

Mary had been watching the store while Maurine was wallowing in the sand with Chris. Maurine did not want to over-extend Mary, as she had concocted a story about a job interview at a beachfront hotel. Maurine knew Mary would not be happy about giving her time off for any reason, certainly not for this.

Following an idyllic hour of giggling, kissing, and teenage philosophizing, Maurine and Chris dusted the sand from their clothing and retraced their steps back to the Promenade. Chris proceeded to walk Maurine toward Joe's Tap. Chris was not bold enough to hold Maurine's hand while going through town. This was point on which she concurred. There were a number of things that they mutually decided could wait, barely!

The next day, Chris came by the store for his daily pretzel rod fix. Maurine grinned as he opened the screen door and entered; there was no air conditioning.

"Hey Maurine, I have something for you," he announced. She gazed at him with youthful inquisition but said nothing. From his pocket, Chris pulled out a box that could have a diamond ring or some other exquisite jewel in it. Maurine was overwhelmed with curiosity and anticipation. He offered Maurine the box, not tipping his hand as to its contents.

She looked at it with a blush; from the consideration Chris showed, and a puzzlement of what it was. Maurine, not one used to receiving many presents, opened it.

It wasn't a diamond or some other precious stone. "It's the medal I won at the Cape Island Invitation track meet last May. It is silver for second place," he gushed. It was Chris's first individual and proudest varsity medal in track. Thus, it was veritably inestimable in its value, and had the seminal impact of a flawless report card.

Maurine cried at the significance and the affection with which she felt he offered. By the next day, she had a silver chain around her neck with the medal dangling. Their nip at puppy love had just grown to the size of Benito.

Chris continued to frequent the store throughout summer with all of the reasons in the world to smile. He and Maurine really liked each other. So what do these aspiring first-time lovers do at this age? They go to different schools. The fact that they were enrolled in different high schools may have been a blessing. Not being around each other all the time, allowed for them to immerse in other pastimes. They were not guided by the innate temptations they inexorably presented to the other. For Chris it was sports; for Maurine it was Mary delegating more chores around Joe's Tap and the little store. The glowing embers of fascination for each other stayed lit throughout the year. However, Mary had other ideas. She was storing water to make sure those embers did not grow into an out-of-control conflagration.

Mary subscribed to a demented idea that whoever "possessed" Maurine, controlled Mo. Almost from birth, Maurine was an adhering agent for Mary to cling to Mo. Mary sought to manipulate the world Maurine traveled, in order to keep a handle on Mo. She did not want Mo to divert his attention away from the bar or herself. As long as Maurine was near, Mo would be too! Originally, it was Mo's wife who was banished. Mary coordinated a raid on Helena's mailbox when the time change for the custody hearing was delivered. Now, perversely enough, it was Chris's turn. This made sense only to Mary, but she viewed Chris as a threat. Mary also influenced the Catholic school with her "donations," while not considering the abuse to which Maurine was subjected. After nearly fifteen years without having a say in her life, Maurine was fully poised to protect this portion of it. Now, Mary and Maurine were on a collision course, facing all-out war.

Chapter Seven *Ella*

As a scholar, Ella's success was not any more stellar than Antonio's. Mary pressured the nuns at the elementary school to pass Ella from grade to grade, but offered no demands upon Ella to improve; nor did she seek a remedy for her shortcomings. Additionally, Ella's grades for her first couple years of high school were alarmingly poor. Her reading capability was closer to a fourth grade level. If Ella had been born a generation later, her problem might have been diagnosed as dyslexia. She took ribbing in school for being a "dummy," and in the bar as a "dimwit." Such characterizations were overstated. Ella was smart enough to know the limits of her talent, and showed well in Bible stories and religion. Ella had given thought to being a nun. One of the teachers, a nun, told her that there was a lot of reading involved and she should "find something else to pursue." She could not think of anything else.

Maurine got more attention than Ella at home and in school. Maurine was far more demonstrative and perceptive. Either due to her meek temperament or her dubious parentage, Ella's contribution to Joe's Tap was shamefully under-appreciated, and otherwise, ingloriously dismissed.

Ella had the same financial constrictions that Maurine did, and was offered the same "salary" at the bar. Ella was aware of Maurine's commercial enterprise but neither knew the extent of it, nor was she involved in it. Nevertheless, Ella still had the need for a stronger financial base. Money was a topic that brought hand-to-hand combat from Mary, and Mary would win. Mary had hit Ella more than once when the issue was aired. Ella stopped asking. Now a teenager, it did not take Ella long to figure things out. During slow times in the bar, when Joe would go to the bathroom, she would take five dollars from the cash register. This happened usually once a week. She knew how long Joe would be gone and how long Mary would be out of the bar. The five bucks would cover lunch money in school, sanitary napkins, and a dollar she would put in the plate at church. For Ella, if starvation were not her prime motivation, she would not have done it. Too often she and Maurine had gone to school hungry, with no more cash than to get a dime soda along with a nickel for a bag of potato chips.

As Joe was getting older his eyesight was betraying him as much as Mary and Mo were. His disheartening loss of vision could easily be traced back to World War II, where he was exposed to syphilis while in Europe. His case went un-diagnosed and untreated until just before he was discharged, more than two years after his initial exposure. Joe's reluctance to be treated, and the idea that field penicillin was meant for those actually wounded in combat, exacerbated its spread. This condition probably contributed to Mary romantically distancing her from him not long after his return, but it surely had something to do with his retreating vision.

By five o'clock on most weekdays, Joe could be seen sitting on the side porch of the taproom with a couple of his companions, listening to a portable radio for the horse racing results. His buddies would read the *Racing Form* while he nestled the radio to his ear. Jinx was usually Joe's trusted eyes on the side porch when perusing the racing sheets. They were amateur handicappers with occasional victories and endless arguments. But they were serious gamblers.

One of Maurine's tasks was to call Joe's bets into his bookie. Horse racing was only one form of wagering that Joe participated. He gave and took points in football and basketball and played the odds in boxing. He had neither been to the track nor seen a game of any kind for probably ten years, even on television. Maurine would phone the bookmaker and place the bets from the small store. She translated Joe's quirky annotations, and sometimes-strange markings, that went all over the notepaper. The original bookie they routinely dealt with got arrested and was charged with illegal gambling and bookmaking. Joe couldn't see very well, but meant to write such that no one but Maurine could decipher the scribbles. It was an effective system.

Word in the bar was that there were stings in place to corral bookmaking action in New Jersey. Joe, through his sources, found another bookie. To avoid any detection or wiretaps, Joe made sure that Maurine called from the pay phone in the train depot next to Joe's Tap, on her way to the store. This was not an orthodox chore for most teenage girls, but then what else is new?

One fortunate feature about a seashore resort is that the beach season runs concurrent with the time school is in recess. Imagine that! From Memorial Day to Labor Day shore towns grow from sleepy listless burghs to kinetic seats of varied pleasure and leisure. It is a time of year that is essential for community survival with the regeneration of beach traffic. The populations of those communities multiply many times over during this period. The weather is a prime partner in the psychological disposition and the commercial success of the resort towns.

Periodic summer rains chase bathers into the bars, restaurants, and souvenir shops for a splurge of unanticipated spending. On one rain-threatened summer day in 1965, Ella was doing busy work that Mary had instructed her to get done in the bar. Except for going to regular Mass, Ella's entire summer world did not extend beyond the bar. Only as a small child could Ella remember going to the beach which rested but three blocks away.

Mary consistently put in a couple hours at the candy store before turning it completely over to Maurine, who was also at the store; Mary would then return to the bar. Joe was handling Joe's Tap. Mo had a construction job.

Following a brief run of retreating bathers from a climaxing lightning barrage and a heavy ten-minute shower, the sun returned the early afternoon bar cadence back to its customary languor, as customers disappeared to the beach. On this afternoon, Joe did something that had been weighing on his mind for too long of a time. Ella dutifully swept sand from the vacated taproom floor. And amid the lingering aroma of draft beer and sunscreen lotion, Joe beckoned Ella into a refrigerated pantry. This was ostensibly for her to help him find something. Knowing that he would have the place to run with just Ella on board until Mary returned at about three-fifteen, one-and-a-half hours away, Joe sexually assaulted Ella. He raped her. She was sixteen; he was fifty-three.

Ella offered only momentary, confused, resistance and then cooperated. Joe was her uncle, landlord, boss, father figure, and besides Mo, the only man whom she was not afraid. She had no boys flirting with her like Maurine did. And now, with bizarre authority, Joe was showing her that she was worthwhile. Joe overpowered her. Not wanting to bruise her or rip any of Ella's clothing, Joe grabbed her from the rear. He proceeded to fondle Ella's mature, fully formed breasts and talked to her like she was a child. Joe worked Ella's panties down as he clutched her tightly. For Joe, he was in total arousal mode and went at Ella with little reservation. Ella relaxed and submitted herself to him. Her choosing to do this had as much to do with her having something different going on in her dreary day other than sweeping sand. For Joe, he cultivated a companion borne from an insensitive, incestuous position of dominance; not a lover developed through respect and caring. The conquest wasn't like he could raise the flag on Iwo Jima or he was holding a winning trifecta ticket. Ella was defenseless prey, and he was a famished predator.

Joe sternly implied that she was responsible for what transpired, and that he would tell everyone just that, if she ever opened her mouth about it. He made the point of telling Ella that he would especially advise the priest of her shameful influence on him. Short on self-esteem and confidence, and long on Catholic guilt, she complied. The thought of living her current life in a more entrenched condition of perpetual derision by Mary and Carmen, and her after-life in a state of eternal spiritual damnation was more than Ella needed to contemplate. She carried her secret into the confessional at church with the same muted conviction as she did everywhere else. Joe dominated Ella's will and her body. Their tryst endured the summer without disruption.

Chapter Eight *Bloody Mary*

C hris bounced a basketball on his way to the courts. His thoughts were on getting his corner jump shot perfected, and seeing Maurine afterwards. Sometimes he day-dreamily saw himself mutating into a hybrid Oscar Robertson and Sidney Poitier, like a comic book super-hero might. He saw himself as a suave leading man that could score against any defense. But some days were not meant to be a reward for being born. On this sweat-drenching afternoon, as fate would have it, Mary walked from the opposite direction headed for the store. Chris had only a nodding rapport with Mary, and figured to nod as they passed. She would occasionally drive by in her old black Fleetwood and Chris would nod. He politely nodded this time as their eyes met. Mary did more than nod.

"Chris, I want to talk to you," she said glumly.

"Yeah?"

She got right to the point. "I want you to stop seeing Maurine," she said as distinctly as a rusty nail penetrating one's foot. "I want her to finish school!"

Chris was not anticipating this conversation. Now fully awakened from his daydream but not fully aware of what she meant, replied, "I want her to finish school too. Maurine never mentioned anything about quitting school." The only thing that was making an impression on Chris was the jiggling of Mary's second chin. Never had he been this close to her before, and he determined she was not particularly good looking and that she was definitely fat.

Chris soberly stood there in blank teenage bewilderment. How would Sidney handle this?

"You don't understand what I mean so I am going to tell you so you can," she continued. "She is too young to be involved with a boy like you, and she sure as hell don't need no babies!"

Chris is stunned by Mary's mandate, as he was positive that he and Maurine had done nothing to affect a baby. He did not think squeezing a boob a year ago could create a baby. His naïve efficacy was jolted into the reality of what he and Maurine had done, or at least wanted to do. Damn, maybe Mary was right! Maurine was about to be a junior. Chris had a year of high school remaining and then he was determined to go to college. He continued on, to work on his jump shot, but was leery about seeing Maurine later.

Maurine previously had a similar conversation but was less affected by hers than Chris was with his. Maurine and Mary had a sustained history of confrontation, and Maurine did not cower in that one. For Maurine, Chris was a genuine keeper, and Mary was not allowed to get in the way. Mary, on the other hand, hoped that Chris would be more intimidated by her than she knew Maurine was, if she rattled her saber at the proper angle. Mary was not a gracious competitor, and was not bound to Marquis of Queensbury rules in a struggle that she might lose. She would fight dirty, and she would win.

When Chris passed the store, he would look for Maurine, but would not enter. On one occasion she came out the door and said something, not in a demanding way, but more like "hey, I am still here, where are you?" Maurine had no idea what was going on with Chris. The medal remained around her neck; she removed it only to bathe.

After coming home from work not long after his dress-down by Mary, Chris got a more profound shock when his father out of the clear blue said, "Dammit boy, I want you to stop seeing Mary Di Cicco's daughter!" Chris did not even know that his father was aware of his seeing Maurine. Did Mary get to his dad? Within the span of a week, Chris was admonished to dump the "love" of his life and his now best friend from the highest of all worldly powers, Mary *and* his Dad. He did not argue but mused to himself, "Mary Di Cicco's *daughter*? Love is a lot easier watching it on television. Man, I can't wait for football practice to start!"

Joe's Tap had hosted some wedding receptions over the years. It was large enough to handle a modest sized event. They would hire out for a caterer, or just have snacks, depending on the interest of the parties. A close friend of Mary and Carmen had a daughter who desired getting married. The daughter was twenty-seven-years-old and already had four children. She was pregnant at the moment. The mother was having considerable difficulty finding a minister, church, or venue to have the ceremony. She shared this with Carmen who passed it on to Mary. Mary offered Joe's Tap to hold the wedding. The offer was happily accepted and the date was set. The Saturday after Labor Day was selected, at three o'clock in the afternoon. The reception would be catered and open to all. This was big news in the bar. Hand-written notices, ornately lettered by Maurine, were placed around the bar. And some invitations were mailed out on a personal basis.

For the regulars, the prospect of this event and its contributing implications took on a simultaneous sacred and comical presence. But the real coup was that the guys could get their drinking started a couple hours earlier with a four o'clock start time; cash bar. Now they just had to locate a minister that who liked to drink, or at the least, did not mind conducting business in a taproom.

On the day of the wedding, Joe's Tap looked like a cathedral. Transitioned that morning with a volunteer work force, that were friends of the family, the stools and chairs were arranged like church pews. The bar tables were covered with a series of white tablecloths. Someone sent a couple flower arrangements. A borrowed red carpet was rolled out for the bride's entrance. They did not have a piano in the bar, but a local music teacher offered to play the accordion. The bride's family minister relented from his previous position and decided to conduct the ceremony. However, he did not relent on having the service in his church.

Ella and Maurine doubled as ushers and bridesmaids, and were dressed smartly. Maurine ordered outfits from the Sears catalog for Ella and herself. These were tasteful semi-formal dresses. Maurine let Ella to pick the color she liked. She chose lilac.

Mo, Antonio, and Joe stood behind the bar in white-jacketed tuxedos; they used the tuxes when they did contract bar tending at yacht clubs, or occasional special catered events. The ceremony went off without any problems. The bride's children sat under the neon Cutty Sark sign, and were cutely dressed. They behaved themselves. One was a charming five-year-old flower girl.

Judge, who was a devout churchgoer, provided the sartorial hit of the day. Donning his black pin-striped vested suit, chained pocket watch, derby hat, and walking cane, Judge easily out-distanced anybody else who thought they might claim "best dressed" honors. As if his fabulous attire was not classy enough, he finished it off with a pair of white spats. All of the regulars cleaned up for the occasion, but Judge stole the show. Ella giggled that Judge looked like advertising icon Mr. Peanut.

The accordion marked the processional. The bride was given away by her younger brother. The new couple beamed. After the ceremony, pictures were taken inside the bar and outside with the train station and an idle train serving as the background. The radiant bride wore a white gown, as it was her first marriage. Being seven months pregnant and in the white gown, provided fodder for some of the regulars to poke some fun at a serious and solemn ceremony. Ella caught the bouquet, just in front of an aggressive Bertha, whereupon her mother, Carmen, immediately snatched it from her. The bride and groom drove off to a honeymoon at a local hotel for the night. The children went home with their grandmother. This was one of Joe's Tap's more meaningful and tasteful offerings. Friends of the family kept the bar festivities rocking and with the regulars drank beyond the midnight hour. Overall, it was a long happy day.

The one dubious casualty of the event was the marriage itself. It lasted all of seven weeks, or at about the same time the baby was born. What timing! The husband determined the baby wasn't his, and was told as much by a number of sources, including a man who claimed to be the real father. Noting the baby looked just like that other guy, the new husband walked out of the marriage feeling wounded and betrayed. The disintegration of the marriage was just one more topic for analysis and dissection for the regulars of Joe's Tap. "I told you so," seemed to be a common refrain.

Chapter Nine *Anxiety*

Amazingly, Maurine had a reliable liquor selling business into her junior year at Stella Maris High School. Her weekly income was substantial and the clients were quite zealous about sustaining her contribution. In the three plus years of having her business, all of the players had been respectful of the enterprise and mindful of not getting caught at home. It all came to a screeching halt when members of the school's boys' soccer team were discovered to have booze on a road trip. As stoic as the athletes tried to endure, one of the fellows cracked under the questioning and word got out that Maurine was the heretofore unnamed supplier.

After considerable investigation by the school and the church all of the focus zeroed in on Maurine. Ultimately, the only thing that saved her from permanent expulsion was that the other people involved were offspring of some prominent Cape May/Wildwood families. The parents did not think that the school's only black student depicted as a "scapegoat" would solve things, for pointed fingers could find a way back to their kids. There would not be a seller if there was not a buyer, and many of these kids had been buying for a long time.

Overall, the incident was treated like it never happened. For a private Catholic school surviving on tuition and a solid reputation, the publicity this episode would draw could be nigh on fatal. The condition for Maurine's reinstatement, after a one day suspension and an irate Mo visiting the principal, was that she not peddle booze to the students again. That was the end of it. Some of those kids had to take alcohol counseling. She was not remanded to counseling. What was the point to counsel a person whose home was a bar?

Ella started the school year along with Maurine but was overtaken with an illness shortly thereafter. She had a perceptive weight gain and was crying even more than she used to. She had always been overweight and she always cried; no one gave much thought to it. One day she asked Maurine if she had any money. She wanted to go to the doctor. After the obligatory questions from Maurine about why she didn't ask her mother or Mary, Ella broke into tears.

Both Maurine and Ella knew that Mary and Joe had a searing aversion to doctors and hospitals. As they had parents and siblings die in hospitals, their mind set was that hospitals were a place "where you go to die!" Maurine thought that this was Ella's resistance for approaching the elders and understood this. However, Ella simply wanted to visit a doctor without adult intervention.

Maurine seeing that Ella was distraught, and had witnessed this on numerous occasions in the past, focused on giving Ella a trustworthy support. Based on observing Ella's behavior and penchant for recent illness, she thought Ella's symptoms sounded much like what women in the bar talked about when they were having a baby. How could that be possible? Maurine was holding her breath on that call. In the recesses of her mind, she thought if Ella was pregnant, that her father, God forbid, was *not* the father. Ella had never really engaged Maurine in such a conversation as pregnancy, and Ella probed Maurine on many topics. She and Ella had only superficial talks about sex, but nothing really heavy. Maurine picked up her basic sex education overhearing conversations in the bar. Maurine considered, "Maybe she had mono or something!"

For all Ella cared, or knew, birds and bees were no more than flying animals. Her illness was genuine, and so was her ignorance. Ella was far more sheltered than Maurine had been, and becoming a mother was not part of her goals. Actually, Ella had no goals. Her only serious purpose was to get through a day without Mary or Joe making her life any more depressing; she could rarely avoid either of them on most days.

Maurine said, "Sure I have money for you to go to the doctor. I'll go with you." Maurine and Ella did a miserable job of hiding their anxieties, but they had worked through each other's problems all of their lives, but nothing like this. Ella did not even relate to her malady like Maurine did, but knew that she did not like the way she felt.

Maurine decided that instead of taking the school bus home to Cape May, they would go to a doctor in Wildwood, where the school was located, immediately after class. She sought to avoid detection by prying eyes in Cape May. Ella checked-in with the receptionist and she and Maurine sat in the waiting room. Gentle music from the local FM radio station played in the room among the sterile antiseptic smell. Ella and Maurine picked through a couple magazines without any focused predisposed objective. They were passing the time until the nurse called Ella. An old man came out of the examining room. Ahead of them were a mother and her agitated six-year-old son, who were promptly summoned. Both girls put their magazines down. Maurine clasped Ella's hand but said nothing. Now was not a good time to yuck things up. Before seeing the mother and little boy come out, the nurse surprisingly called Ella's name disrupting a moment of pure teenage bonding. Ella and Maurine embraced and then separated. Ella followed the nurse and Maurine sat back in her seat, fumbling with an old edition of the *Saturday Evening Post*.

Moments after Ella went in, the mother and son came out with the boy showing more composure than he did before. The office was quite still except for the occasional ringing of the phone slicing through the easy music. It was five minutes until four and no one else had come in. At four-twenty, Ella came out with the nurse and summoned Maurine to pay the bill. Maurine sprang to her feet and went to the window. Ella stood next to her with a sheepish grin of relief and embarrassment. Maurine paid for the exam and departed with Ella for the bus stop. They were in a rush to get there to catch the four-thirty bus to Cape May. Since they had not checked in with anyone at the bar, they figured to be on that bus. They hurried each other to the stop and nothing else was said. The bus was coming and they were waiting for it when it arrived. It will take the bus about forty-five minutes to traverse the five miles, after touring the rural areas transitioning into population centers, between Wildwood and Cape May.

Maurine began, "OK, what's up?"

Ella sighed and hunted for words. After a couple flamed-out attempts to reply, wound up saying, "I am going to have a baby in March."

After a moment of genuine shock Maurine said, "Darn, that's going to be a bunch of 'hail Marys!' I hope it's a Pisces. I get along well with Pisces (Chris was a Pisces), or used to! So you gonna tell me who the lucky daddy is?" Maurine tried to be witty and not too judgmental at a time she knew that Ella must be crushed. She also wanted get past the angst of Mo possibly being the dad.

With Maurine's inquiry about the father, Ella's demeanor changed from one of relief to dread when she reflected back on what Joe had told her. She could not speak anymore, and coiled next to Maurine. Maurine was scared because she just knew Ella's silence must mean it's Mo. Finally, they both sat back and watched the afternoon brightness dissolve into dusk. Maurine doesn't probe Ella. Ella will say what she needs to say when she is ready.

Chapter Ten *Halloween*

S ome of the Victorian homes had transformed into picturesque multi-unit bed and breakfasts. They were not the shabby old structures in need of a coat of paint, but refurbished architectural charms. The summers saw these newly appointed inns gaining in prominence, constantly filled, and brimming with activity. Patrons sipped cocktails and teas on the pleasant porches. The yards were punctuated with full blooming hydrangeas, and beautifully adorned flower beds smothered by dark mulch.

Older non-Victorian buildings were razed to allow for contemporary structures. Every yard, old and new, was a landscaper's canvas. Colorful tulips, crocuses, daffodils, and hyacinths welcomed the spring. Trimmed rose bushes and potted geraniums added a scarlet tinge in the early summer, with gladiolas and marigolds dominating the late summer, and filled the town with color. Chrysanthemums flourished in the autumn. Hedges and shrubs were meticulously tended and shaped. Cape May endured a resurgence of recognition and vitality. Some people had invested large amounts of money for having the privilege to host energized vacationers and pay substantial mortgages. They pursued avenues of extending the season, and bringing traffic to the town after the summer disappeared. There would be no bathing in the ever-roaring, bone-chilling ocean. The Victorian bed and breakfasts sought to be *the* designated objects of post-season commercial focus.

However, not everyone could live off profits generated from tourism. For hired hands the year was split into two seasons: the summer season and the unemployment season. Many residents qualified for compensation from the state by working in the hotels and restaurants during the summer with little expectation of landing fall-winter work of any consequence after October. Unemployment was a valued off-season revenue source.

For Halloween, the girls decorated Joe's Tap with orange and black bunting, and had some hand-carved jack-o-lanterns with candles flickering inside, spaced along the bar. Maurine did the handiwork on the pumpkins. This was an extension of the artistic interest she was growing to like, and for which she was developing varied talents. Joe's Tap was in the midst of its Halloween weekend spruce-up. Costumes were welcomed, but optional.

Although people at Joe's sensed something was going on with Ella, she remained silent on issuing any clue that would indict her as corrupting Joe. He still found time to assault her. Maurine was holding Ella's secret, protecting Ella and perhaps shielding her father. She had yet to find out the name of the father. Ella could not maintain total secrecy much longer as her figure was obviously expanding.

As the evening passed, patrons filled Joe's Tap, and bar orders were heavy. Mo and Joe tended a crowded bar; Carmen had the tables. An out of town female acquaintance of Mo's sat at the bar, dressed in a slinky beige Pocahontas type of outfit. She wore a red sequined mask. Behind the mask was a light skinned Puerto Rican woman with two large braids that plunged on either side of her obviously nice looking face. From beneath a red headband, with a single white feather upright in the back of it, she capped her sexy, native-American, Halloween visual. Mo found time to devote particular attention to this woman in her late 20s. Mary was not in the bar; she was away visiting a younger sister in Florida who had three children, and whose husband was dying of cancer.

An ominous full moon commanded the Saturday night sky. The Halloween festivities brought out a larger than usual crowd, fully intent on having a good time. As customers filed in, they were met with the thump-thumping beat of the jukebox. Cigarette smoke clung to the dim lights above the bar like wadded cotton puffs suspended from Smoker's Heaven. Joe was hustling to fill the orders. Mo was hustling the woman. By now, the woman had removed her sequined mask. This woman was the corporal antithesis of Mary, and Mo was fixated on her. Her figure was trim and was superbly accented by her tight outfit. She had no wrinkles or dangling flab. She was engaging, with a playful bite to her conversation. Mo's feet got stuck in place while chatting with her, even as customers requested service.

Joe's eyesight may not have been too good, but he knew when his help was dragging on him. And because his eyes weren't great, his hearing had become more intense. Joe thought he heard Mo say something like, "Hell no baby, she don't rule me. I am my own man. She means nothing to me!"

Joe said, "Come on Mo; let's get those guys down there!" He gestured to three fishermen, brilliantly disguised as…fishermen, with empty glasses toward Mo's end of the bar. Joe somehow recognized when patrons needed service.

The young woman, with her voice piercing through the clatter, said to Mo, "Well I guess her husband doesn't own you either, huh!" Joe heard this part clearly and totally lost his composure. His face reddened with anger, and his mind blanked of any rational bearing. Mo remained entertained by the woman. Mo had still not made a move to take care of customers looking to spend money.

Joe slid the tray of beers he just poured to Carmen for delivery. His vision was cruelly blurred, but he knew exactly where everything in the bar was located. Even his penchant for making correct change was exemplary. He walked past Mo, who was still leaned in to talk to the woman across the bar, and sought a location beneath the cash register.

Joe pulled a pistol from a "hiding spot" and pointed it at Mo.

"You black son of a bitch, I know what you and Mary do. I have known that for a long time. But I am not going to listen to you disrespect her while I feed you and your kid. You're not doing your job, and I am tired of all of it!"

Joe did not seem expressly ticked about Mo not pulling his weight, because Mo was always there and had proven his allegiance to Joe's Tap; or even talking to the girl, because Mo always flirted. These were the espoused catalysts for his eruption and probably stung Joe at a busy time when he was most susceptible to irritation. Mo knew that Joe could get nuts at times if he caught an employee stealing or not collecting for drinks. More than reacting to Mo's shoddy effort, Joe countered as if he was truly defending Mary's honor. Go figure!

As the customers became aware of the unfolding drama, Halloween took on, perhaps appropriately so, an absolutely supernatural persona. The chatter stopped cold. The jukebox, which had a mind of its own, continued playing oblivious to the commotion.

The only thing moving was the cigarette smoke dancing toward the ceiling to the lovers' anthem *My Girl* of the Temptations. Everything else stood suspended in wacky disarray. Mo getting wasted by Joe was not something patrons got to see every day.

Altercations were an occupational certainty, but Joe was the usual arbiter and peacemaker. Mo had never seen Joe go for the gun, which Mo knew was there, and he also knew it was loaded. He decided to remain calm and not add kerosene to Joe's already inflamed psyche. At the sight of the pistol, "Pocahontas" promptly bolted for the door, leaving her mask *and* purse on the bar. Joe was in full focus of everyone, but Mo was the only one in the line of potential fire. Mo was the only one facing down the barrel of a war souvenir, German Lugar. Many wriggled to get a closer view. Some bailed to the floor, others sprinted for the exits. Yet *nobody* trusted the aim of a crazed, blind, white man.

"Put the gun down, Joe!" A woman yelled.

"It's about time he did this," voiced one man.

"I gotta get a better look," said another.

"Did he say, '*black* son of a bitch?'" A woman asked, through the reluctant murmur of the apprehensive crowd.

Mo, still faced the gun and an incensed Joe, tried to talk his way out of it. He had on a red T-shirt that said "Philadelphia Phillies National League Champs 1964." He also wore a red cap with a white script P. The irony in the moment was that the Phillies did not win the pennant the year before. Mo is now hoping that he did not meet the same fated demise as the '64 Phillies. He called upon the only thing he thought Joe might relate to in this spot. He knew that ducking or running would not work.

"Wait a minute now Joe, let me buy you a drink, and I'll buy a round for everybody!" This was no time to get into a debate about his comparative value to the bar, or who paid Maurine's way. Right now, his luck seemed to be working as well as it did for the damned baseball team.

Mo's proposition did not take long to make its mark. "Hey Joe, Mo said 'set 'em up.' Get me a Jack and Coke!" hollered a brave customer, not looking to pass on a free drink, nor lose a sponsor willing to buy him one.

"Let me have a Seven and Seven!" A woman demanded.

Within seconds, everyone got the idea, and was shouting for action on Mo's offer.

"Joe, get me one of those 'white Russians,'" hollered Poison Sumac. She opted not to put her dentures in as part of her Halloween costume as popular comedienne Jackie "Moms" Mabley, "and my friend Bertha here, will have a black man with some money!" She said in her gruff Moms Mabley voice. Even the most uptight of the patrons found that funny.

Joe's face was still a raging crimson or about the same color as Mo's shirt, finally heard the imploring bar crowd and told Mo to "get back to work!" Mo in considering his options, recognized an acceptable deal for him, and promptly bought a round for the crowded house. Joe slid the gun under the bar from where he got it, and he and Mo got back to the business of selling drinks. Customers who were waiting on the sidewalk for the sound of Joe busting a cap in Mo, got the "all clear" from someone inside, and returned to talk about the events that sent Joe over the edge, and get their gratuitous libations.

Although he remained living at Joe's Tap, Mo told Joe that he had tired of bartending and was going to concentrate on his earth-moving business. He did not say it, but Mo did not need Joe as much as Joe needed him, and it was evident that Joe resented Mo. This was not an illustrious time around Joe's Tap.

By mid-November on a Tuesday, Chris sent through Antonio, a message to Maurine. Antonio was in his sixth year of high school, but seemed he was still not on a serious pace to graduate. Antonio found that high school clouded draft board detection, as fighting escalated in Southeast Asia. Chris was hoping that Maurine would go to the football banquet and dance with him after the final game. He needed to know because the game and dance were but a scant week and a half away. Joe's Tap had never advanced beyond having a public pay telephone. He had kept putting off trying to contact Maurine. He feared calling because he wanted nothing to do with Mary, and she might answer the phone. Antonio promised delivery of a sealed letter. In the letter, Chris even suggested that Maurine call him and added his phone number, which he knew that she knew by heart, even though she had never called. The aspect of Chris's life that kept the still-splendid spark for Maurine was bundled in apprehension and perplexity. He wanted so much to be around her, and still could not understand what made Mary such an ogre. He'd take one more shot.

On Thursday, two days later, Antonio located Chris in the crowded, fast-paced cafeteria. Chris sat with some football buddies. Antonio told Chris, "Maurine can't make the dance," and handed him a package.

Chris, defiantly not showing his frustration and disappointment, took the package. It was an unadorned brown paper bag. At least she sent him something. "Thanks, Antonio. Later, man!" Chris opened the package. He didn't want to let on about his dismay, but his silver track medal was in the package. He felt a tear swell in his eye. It wasn't even silver anymore. It was tatty brown from Maurine wearing it. It wasn't *real* silver after all; it might not even have been medal. Who cares, he now had *gold* medals to give girls if he wanted to. But Maurine finally let him know what he meant to her, and in this meet he did not place.

To add salt to Chris's wounded heart, Cape Island High got spanked by Wildwood High 33-14, his final high school football game. Chris cracked a rib, did not play in the second half, and went stag to the banquet/dance trussed in a wrap-around binding. Damn, what would Sidney do?

Chris survived his rib injury, and the perceived snub inflicted by Maurine. He was soon helping the varsity basketball team, despite doing a poor imitation of Oscar Robertson. He was not the star, and was not the team high scorer. He toiled under the basket for rebounds. He had fouled out of five of the first eight games and averaged seven points and eleven rebounds. Maurine who up to now had not been allowed any extracurricular school activities by Mo and Mary, didn't immediately come home from school the January day when Cape Island High played at Stella Maris. She stayed in Wildwood for the afternoon. She hung around the school library until 4:30, catching up on homework and daydreaming. She ate at a nearby diner, and was in the school gym early for the 6:30 junior varsity game. The noise and excitement were fantastic. She had never been to any kind of a sporting event before. During the jayvee game she saw Chris sitting with his varsity teammates before they went in to dress for their game. She walked over to say hello. They were happy to see each other, but the coach called the team to get ready for the game before any explanations were traded. She anticipated a scolding by Mary for not showing up at the bar. But she just had to see what Chris looked like in his basketball outfit.

He was "gorgeous." Maurine stayed and watched the first quarter of the varsity game, but she had to leave to catch a bus for Cape May. If she had pursued it, she could have probably hitched a ride home, but she was not comfortable asking anyone. Chris's father and brother were two of the faces in the crowd.

Chris was in the process of having the game of his life. At the end of the first quarter he had a Big O-like twelve points (two of his baskets were corner jump shots), eight rebounds, and only one foul. Cape Island was up 23-8, riding Chris's spirited play.

Watching Chris play basketball was the neatest thing she had ever done in high school. But more than getting a glimpse at Chris, for the first time Maurine became aware that there was life beyond class. Kids from both schools were hollering, clapping, yelling, and cheering. She did too. She wanted more of that. Yet, she could not do that if she remained at Joe's Tap.

During the quarter break, Chris's eyes followed Maurine as she put her coat on and walked out the exit. In the end, Cape Island won 61-59, but Chris's totals were fourteen points, twelve rebounds, and he fouled out. Evidently, his game disappeared the same time Maurine did. Neither Oscar Robertson nor Sidney Poitier could inspire him when Maurine walked out the door.

Chapter Eleven *Derailments*

B enito would relax by the back door of Joe's Tap, and occasionally got up and peeked into the bar. He was conspicuously visible but left the customers to enjoy themselves. Benito could show his temper when needed. A snarling, resolute Benito thwarted intrusion to any off-limits part of Joe's. He was the bar's irrevocable security officer and full-time bouncer. Benito's assumed responsibilities included rat patrol. He was the exterminator. No rodent would get a second chance to see the light of day with Benito around. He was more ruthless than a cat. Benito found sport in eliminating rats and mice. As big as he was, he stealthily stood in the shadows and pounced.

Benito had also evolved into being the Joe's Tap mascot. Maurine had gotten the bar to have a likeness she sketched of Benito printed on the bar's coasters and napkins. Benito was the logo for Joe's Tap. Neither Ella nor Maurine could remember life without Benito until that Christmas.

Benito died on Christmas day, just before the turn into a troubled year. Benito was old and no one exactly knew for sure how old. Benito just showed up at the bar one day and never left. In his heyday, Benito looked like what the dog on *Lassie* would look like if she popped steroids.

Benito was no angel either; his lifestyle was not unlike the adults at Joe's. In various homes around the Joe's Tap area, his numerous offspring, strongly engendering a mixed-collie breeding, carried on his legacy.

By the spring of 1966, Ella had given birth to a baby boy, Jason. He was a Pisces, born on March 20. Ella *never* gave up the name of the father; it was impeccably certain that it was not Mo. Because of the suspicions those at the bar had regarding the baby's father, and most of them were correct, Mary demanded that Ella find someplace else to live. Ella and the baby were unceremoniously shipped out of the bar.

With information from Maurine, the priest in the parish put two and two together, and intervened. He visited the bar and helped transition Ella and the baby. Ella and her child moved in with a couple which she knew from the church, and resided on a small farm in rural, but nearby, Cold Spring. The woman had been Ella's Sunday school teacher when she was younger. Ella had no suitcase. She carried two Sunday outfits on hangers and three shopping sacks, her life's accumulation of clothing and keepsakes. There were even fewer baby things. Ella was in full crying mode. Although Ella did not recognize it at the moment, being thrown out of the bar was a fortuitous sanction for her. She was forced to grow up. Ella was too upset to understand much of this, as so many new things were happening without much orientation. She wasn't prepared for any of it. She soon meshed into a more conventional home life, around people who actually cared. Ella and Jason filled the empty nest of this older couple who were looking to extend their love to someone who might return it.

Garrett and Sharon McCullough were the perfect elixir for Ella's troubles, demeanor, and nature. They were in their late forties, with no hope of having any more children of their own. World War II interrupted their loving marriage that was already showing its share of setbacks. Sharon miscarried two times, once before the war and once afterwards. Garrett was severely burned in an explosion on his bombed ship in the Pacific. He mended, but spent the last year of the war in the hospital while being repaired. Although he received some skin grafts, much of his body simply endured the resulting and disconcerting scar tissue.

Earning a break in life, the McCulloughs were blessed with their son Thane, in 1950; two years after Sharon's second miscarriage. Their belated happiness became perversely tempered, as Thane was diagnosed having the poliovirus at age three; ironically enough, just before the introduction of the Salk vaccine. As Thane got older he would attend Sunday school while Sharon taught the class. He could only walk with the aid of heavy leather and metal braces; a style of walking that could only be described as tortured. His pace was not fluid, and required much strain and effort. The braces clicked and clanked as Thane tried to move. Ella was in the class every week. Maurine was not as meticulous about her attendance, but she was in the class as well.

Thane was small for his age, but was smart and devilishly cute when he wasn't walking. Because of his illness and frail body, the county provided school teachers to come to his home, for his education. Thane's health worsened in 1963, and he died a year later from a degenerated respiratory system, after spending considerable time in an iron lung. He had just reached his fourteenth birthday. It took quite a while for the McCulloughs to adjust and rebound from their loss. Eventually, they considered adoption, and addressed some agencies for ideas. By the time they fully got into a search for children, they were made aware of Ella's hassled situation.

Ella was happy to help in the yard and experienced bucolic daylight. The yard had a pond with ducks and geese next to a garden with beans growing on poles, and tomatoes propped in wire trellises. Chickens were penned in an area where they had far more liberty than the ones at Joe's Tap. As mid-summer approached, she could grab a cantaloupe or a fistful of strawberries for breakfast, or pull a watermelon directly from the vine. The revelation of dew-covered grass squeezing through her shoe-less toes was refreshing. That moist revelation may have also had something to do with the deposits the pet tracking hounds, Mickey and Minnie, left in the yard.

Ella did not have to sleep with one eye open quaking that Joe would sneak into her room. Ella got a job in a deli making sandwiches while Sharon happily tended the infant. Ella walked the two miles in rain, snow, or shine, each way, six days a week. It was the only work she had ever done that was not in Joe's Tap. She did not get rich doing the job she had, with the expenses she incurred taking care of Jason. She earned a real paycheck with her name printed on it. She was proud of the fact that she had a portion of her pay taken out in taxes. She sensed that made her part of a structure that was bigger and stronger than Joe's Tap. Eventually she took a job at a laundry in Wildwood that had insurance benefits. She made a thirty-five minute ride from the stop from where she caught the bus. She continued to work part-time at the deli. She would never again enter Joe's Tap or go to school. Ella was barely seventeen-years-old.

In the aftermath of the near shooting of Mo by Joe, and Maurine trying to distance herself from the morass of her childhood, she moved in with her father's Aunt Rachel. Aunt Rachel's home was in West Cape May, across the tiny bridge, on other side of Island Creek. By now, any evidence of the landfill that used to straddle the creek was gone. The bumpy dirt road had given way to a smoothly paved, asphalt thoroughfare. The creek bed was clean, as minnows and crabs were visible and living unfettered lives. Surrounding marsh grass flourished, and the dismal smell was history.

Maurine had grown to enjoy her life in high school and wanted to stay in the area to complete her senior year, and then escape as soon as she could. There were activities that intrigued her and she wanted to try. The loss of Benito impacted greatly on her. With Ella exiled and Benito gone, she saw no reason to stick around Joe's Tap. She remained the only black in her school. This was an oftentimes regrettable distinction she had tolerated since first grade. She was out of the "black market" liquor sales, snipping an umbilical-like attachment to Joe's Tap. Maurine was gearing up to go to college or art school after her graduation. Her decision to leave Joe's Tap caused yet another serious rift (Mo still smarted over the liquor selling at school) with her father. Maurine also took her first baby steps to find her mother and any possible siblings. Being away from her father took the stifling edge off the personally perplexing mystery of her mother's identity and whereabouts. Maurine now realized enough independence to attempt rudimentary investigation. Was her mother even alive?

Although Aunt Rachel's home in West Cape May was just two miles from Joe's Tap, the omni-present ocean did not dominate the community's economic or ecological viewpoint. West Cape

May declined to wholly capitalize on its proximity to the Atlantic. Although it was minutes away from the Atlantic by walking, it had no shoreline to call its own. West Cape May's chosen identity was far more laid-back than Cape May's. West Cape May took to the concept of "leave things as they are." It had one cop. It purported to have few zoning restrictions and fewer architectural ordinances. It maintained its profile by legislating maximum building height, no liquor licenses, and no construction in designated wetlands parcels. Disdaining the glitter of tourist dollars, its simple blueprint allowed them not to compete against Cape May. They stayed away from the powerful temptation to auction their commercial soul. Maurine sought this less pressurized setting to finish her last year in high school. She could always count on Aunt Rachel for emotional reinforcement and great homemade cookies; neither of which had ever been waiting for her at Joe's Tap.

Aunt Rachel was widowed and in her 70s. She had run a rooming house for many years a block-and-a-half from Joe's Tap. In the summers, the rooming house stayed busy, and Aunt Rachel survived from those proceeds for the entire year. Aunt Rachel was given a take it-or-leave it proposal from the urban renewal authorities a couple years before. Under a threat of "eminent domain," where her property would be condemned and legally taken, she sold her home and business for a seriously undervalued amount and bought a home in West Cape May. Combined with the life insurance from her late husband's death, and money she was fortunate to save over the years, Aunt Rachel otherwise would have been packaged as just another tenant earmarked for recently constructed public housing. Black homeowners in the area had to weigh similar options. In any case, they had to move.

Maurine talked to Aunt Rachel about many things, some of which gave sketchy background on Mo's relationship with her mother. However, there was little else to be learned. Although her insight and sophistication were more advanced from the days canvassing the train station, when she was five, Maurine's drive remained as keen as ever. Sadly, she could no more extend her search as a senior in high school than she could in kindergarten. She had no car, and whatever money she banked was targeted for her entrance into college. Although these precious thoughts stayed with her, she earned her best grades of high school. She was the senior leader of the Pep Club, and even went on the school bus to a couple away basketball games. She was an active member in the Art Club, and went on field trips to museums and galleries. Her future was forming with a bright thought-out scheme. She knew that she wanted to be creative; she knew that she wanted to meet her mother.

The mid-sixties provided the demarcation between the gung-ho post-WWII patriotic mentality that was set in a Cold War framing of the 1950s and early 1960s to a changing of American culture peppered by British influenced pop music and the growing of longer hair. The trend toward things British was popularized by, among others the Beatles and the Rolling Stones. Accompanying the music was a widening of illegal drug usage. Less emphasis was being placed on convention and more substance was given to individual expression. The term "counter-culture" painted over the era in an effort to identify a time that was never previously experienced in America.

The first wave of widespread urban racial unrest awoke a socially complacent America. From 1965 through 1968 there were a series of urban riots where the combustible term "burn, baby, burn" became the maxim for African-American reform.

With simultaneous participation as its cities being in flames, the United States increased its role in Vietnam. Drafted GIs in ever-increasing numbers replaced military "advisors". America's romance with itself was being challenged from within, and the television at Joe's Tap provided the nourishment for lively bull sessions for those locals who offered wayward solutions.

For guys who had gone to segregated schools, and made it through World War II and the Korean War, the move to political and social freedom was accelerating faster than they could comprehend, and something in which they failed to find a comfort level. The younger generation who felt no kinship with a war a half a world away, and had seen a president slain, found their star-spangled judgment chaotically aligned.

That confusing period also built a barrier for an unalterable separation between Chris and Maurine. Neither of them fully understood why the other was not available. They proceeded with their lives like they were diabolically jilted by the other. This was a personal demarcation for them. It would take considerable time before they would realize the truth. For now, they both had lives to live. Lives that carried the blemish of a love lost, and little chance to find someone to live up to their first dramatic brushes with that heart-bending concept.

In a reflective moment, Maurine mailed Chris a wallet-sized cap and gown graduation photo to his Cape May home as a peace offering. There was no response. She wrote on the back of it, simply, "Where are you?" She was not even certain that he received it. They were sensitive yet durable, and fought their separate fights into their young adult years. Overloaded with young adult problems, in an unprecedented time in the country's development, they both moved on. There was so much for both of them to learn, and so little preparation to confront this eye-opening portion of their lives. Sometimes mail doesn't always find its mark!

Chapter Twelve *Filly Freedom*

M aurine's life in the late-sixties was full of stirring awakenings. She graduated from her high school in June of 1967. She had a summer job working at the telephone utility as an operator, in Wildwood. With her eighteenth birthday not for two months, she stood 5 feet 9 inches tall with a curvaceous 148 pounds of untouched femininity. She hoped she would not have to live her regimented Catholic school approach forever. She never intended to become a nun, although Mary suggested it at one time to both Maurine and Ella. She had a whole world to conquer. However, she had to get out of Cape May to find out what the rest of the world held.

Maurine was accepted to Hampton Institute (now University) in Virginia, Howard University, and the Philadelphia College of Art (now University of the Arts). The money that she saved from her liquor sales, plus the money she was earning at the phone company as an operator, was enough to get her through the entire first year, but there were no long-range monies to assure her being able to pay for four years of school.

She asked her father for financial help and he was not so inclined to reach into his pocket this time. What he did offer was to make arrangements for Maurine to live with his cousin in West Philadelphia. He would get her in there for much less than the cost of getting her own apartment, while she went to the art school. However, she would have to pay for her rent and everything else. Overall her preference was probably going to Howard, but she could only go as far as her money took her. She accepted his proposal.

In late August, her father drove her and her things to the cousin's place in Philly for the next phase in her life, the College of Art. Mo extended no other aid for his college-bound daughter. His motoring Maurine to Philadelphia conceivably obscured the detail that he was not providing any money for her education. After all of the years of paying for her Catholic school tuition, he came up substantially short on underwriting her higher education.

For both of them, this drive to Philadelphia was poignant; a reference point for the finality that Maurine was not a little kid any longer. Mo allowed this drive as a concession to his responsibility as a father. Despite the distance that had grown in their relationship her last year in high school, they both felt the emotional tug that her going off to college that any parent and child would on such an exacting occasion. They both were reluctant to expose feelings steeped in dichotomy. Maurine did not cry as her father got in Mary's car returning to Cape May, only because she did not want him to see the tears. For him, it was his only child, and he was fully aware of the significance of her leaving. This too was a somber moment for him. His Little Mo had grown up, but she had already grown away.

Maurine's second cousin Adele welcomed her, but because Mo had greased the skids for Maurine's arrival, Maurine sensed Adele might have been an extension of her father *in absentia*. Adele was forty-one. For Adele, Maurine reminded her of an eighteen-year-old version of herself. She knew the tribulations an attractive young woman, alone in the world, would encounter. Maurine had her own room.

Adele, who wished to be a Broadway show-stopping singer or at least a coveted lounge crooner when she was Maurine's age, was now working the second shift at a clothing factory and singing without particular distinction in a thirty member Baptist church choir. She still had a youthful face and an appealing figure, but knew that neither was destined to endure for much longer.

Maurine approached her new course of life, in the Age of Aquarius, full of idealism and optimism. She enrolled in the art college, and worked at a doughnut shop on the weekends in a waitress uniform. The straightened hair style that she wore during high school had given way to a stylized natural, a modified Afro, that she got from a traditionally men's barber shop. The school uniform she modeled since the first grade was traded for tie-dyed shirts and pre-washed, bell-bottomed jeans. Art students did not get too hung up in conformity. On the few occurrences that she would go to a party with her new college friends, she would stop traffic with her trendy mini skirt and high-heeled shoes--ouch!

Adele had a propensity for socializing. Depending on events and her mood, she would get off work at eleven-thirty at night and go to local pubs with friends or by herself. On occasion she would bring a male suitor into the apartment after such excursions. This caused subtle friction between Adele and Maurine early in their rooming alliance. As Adele's friends became aware of Maurine, Adele's overworked sixth sense told her that Maurine was diverting the attention of those guys. Maurine was usually in bed by eleven, or she could be up working on a project for a class. In neither case did she intrude on Adele's living space nor her consorts. The formerly married Adele failed to fully observe things that way and chafed at Maurine's raw feminine charisma.

Maurine's transition to college life in the big city was far different from the closeted existence of growing up in Joe's Tap and being sequestered in Catholic school most of her life. There was no Mary, and there were no nuns, to stifle the curiosity residing in her, and about a world to which she wanted to be more of a contributing factor.

She did not allow for her current life to get in the way of the preparation for a life after college. Up until now she had yet to determine what that might be. Her classes were demanding with regard to time and curriculum. There was reading of books on art history, style and theory. She had sculpting, etching and sketching classes; each with associated projects to be done. If class work was her only object to overcome, then she could cope easily. She did most of her reading at the college library, but took most of her projects back to her apartment. She was never late with an assignment. And her projects routinely showed creativity and passion.

Within a year of being in Philadelphia, the novelty of her first steps of personal freedom presented challenges she could not have prepared for. Her ventures were not unreasonable considering her age and her lack of urbane practice. The results were perhaps predictable. Some cases proved to be overpowering. But if they were all "learning experiences," Maurine was sitting in kindergarten again.

Chapter Thirteen *Jinx*

C ape May valiantly rolled through storms that challenged the
resolve of the seawall. The will of Cape May with its desire to
survive constantly contested the unfeeling wrath of hurricanes and
tidal flooding. These were almost annual battles against tropical
storms bearing new names with no permanent, clear-cut, winner.
With each powerful gust Cape May found renewed determination
and the necessary resources to fight back. Cape May honed its
strategy for physical and economic survival and cleaned out the
portions of town that failed to contribute to the Victorian image
that had become so crucial in its marketing. It also strengthened
defensive ecological measures in the same bureaucratic swipe.

The area around Joe's Tap began to change its landscape in
dramatic fashion. Edging its way toward the seventies, properties
were being purchased by private developers and speculators, and
hawked by aggressive realtors. The old neighborhood had disappeared,
taking with it much of the multi-ethnic flavor it formerly offered.
Condos and vacation rentals sat where the old houses used to be.
Time's pendulum had swung through the surrounding area with
the refinement of a chain saw in a rain forest. What a grand time
to be a building contractor! Cape May was fully promoting its new
identity, and looked good doing it. For better or worse, it also looked
considerably whiter.

Urban riots continued to rally the thinning number of old-time
regulars of Joe's Tap. Their search was on to find the solution for
America's spreading domestic unrest. The local situation was less
explosive, but equally trying. At the end of the sixties, blacks in

Cape May faced displacement, or eviction to a section that could be called a low-income "reservation," the projects. Properties were being bought up. Blacks were not offered to re-develop, but paid to get out. Like Aunt Rachel, those colorful personalities at Joe's Tap moved on.

New low-rise housing cleaned up the area around Joe's Tap where the chic condos and apartments failed to extend. It presented modern residence for families who fell beneath a certain income strata. Many of the regulars improved their living condition. They were paying rent in older buildings that probably needed elimination anyway. However, it seemed that the new projects were aimed at keeping black folks from encroaching the Montpelier Avenue area or the beachfront. No low income accommodations were built near Montpelier Avenue.

The faces did not necessarily change at Joe's Tap they simply disappeared. Blue Dick inexplicably (drunken malaise?) drowned in the marshes while he was trapping muskrat. His body was not discovered for at least two weeks. Mr. Sid had died of old age, the residue of a hard life of manual labor. Greenie died of lung cancer, a product of almost a life-long addiction of chain-smoking un-filtered cigarettes. Jinx was in and out of hospitals from a liver condition for which he was admonished not to drink or smoke. However, when he was not in the hospital, he was in Joe's Tap, drinking and smoking.

Judge sold his house and rental properties in the area under the ubiquitous threat of "eminent domain" and moved with his wife, into a Camden retirement home. Camden was home to Judge's oldest son.

Judge had a twenty-year career as a bailiff in the county court system. Early on he was a custodian as Greenie once claimed. However Judge had a rock-solid state retirement pension. His family had also run the concessions at the black beach section for forty years until the raging '62 flooding carried all of his equipment from a storm-battered storage shed out into the Atlantic.

Judge would have nightmares about some guys in Spain or Portugal sunning themselves on a beach in Judge's beach chairs or sitting under one of Judge's umbrellas. They were also eating Judge's hotdogs, while they drank bottles of Judge's Royal Crown Cola. All of Judge's equipment and food was a present from the storm. It was also a sign to Judge to get out. Judge woke up when he saw naked girls hop on his inflatable rafts in the Italian Riviera.

Judge got an insurance check for his losses and sold the franchise and licenses to a white investor. He then spent much of his idle time at Joe's Tap. Judge stayed until the end of the month, and then moved. He was now removed and distanced from his friends and familiar atmosphere. Having more money than he could spend, Judge simply sat by his window, overlooking the Delaware River. He moped his last days away wishing he could be at Joe's Tap. He yearned to be on his stool, holding court, next to Jinx and Doc. Judge's former residence and family homestead had also been leveled to house a large gazebo. March band music or Dixieland concerts for the vacationing wanderers looking for something cheap to do in the middle of the week sprang from what used to be Judge's bedroom.

Judge died six months after his relocation. This was from a broken heart, as much as anything. He was buried in Cape May with his derby hat resting on his chest with his cane at his side. The correct time on his watch was set and it was wound for the last time. His spats were buttoned neatly.

Puerto Rican Jesus, who was now a custodian in the high school, had married a local black girl and raised a family. He did not come to the bar as much as he once did. Big Dick, Doc, General, Major, and Clarkie were the incumbent roster of Joe's Tap regulars. To replace Mo, Mary hired a guy named Jerry Strawberry. Mo still lived there and came into the bar, but did not tend bar. Mo would sit with Mary and occasionally got involved in the taproom discussions.

Jerry Strawberry was an easy-going, dark-skinned, black man, in his late twenties. He ventured from North Carolina to Cape May in the early sixties to work in the hotel kitchens during the summers, and lived at Aunt Rachel's rooming house. He spent three years in the Army. Jerry Strawberry served in Vietnam, and saw combat. Upon his discharge, he found his way back to the resort and discovered that Joe's Tap was looking for a full-time bartender. Mary knew Jerry Strawberry and needed a reliable replacement that she could "manage."

When Martin Luther King was murdered in April 1968, the remaining regulars of Joe's Tap convened, in what could be rated an "emergency session" on the highest level. The original black and white television had given way to a newer black and white TV in an era when color was booming. The images were clearer than before, but the issues had never lost focus.

"I bet you it was J. Edgar Hoover, who killed King!" Clarkie supposed. "We would have been integrated a long time ago, if it wasn't for him; they say he killed Kennedy!"

"God, I hope it wasn't somebody black who did it; like those guys who got Malcolm X!" Big Dick plead.

"Does it matter? Now King is a martyr, and he's got all you people worked up. This is going to scare the government, and put you back in chains!" Jinx claimed. "They did it to the Japanese during the war. Locked 'em up just for being Japs. I'd feel real bad coming in here with just Joe and Mary to drink with!" Jinx's drawl punctuated his alcohol-induced illogic.

Joe hollered, "Jinx you know you shouldn't be drinking anyway. I'd cut you off if I thought the bar could survive!"

"Jinx, these cities are burning up. I hope you are not right, because the Man is going to get mad pretty soon, and start rounding black folks up," agreed Big Dick, as he found merit in Jinx's statement. "It's not like we can hide anywhere! Black folks can't hide from the government. This country ain't big enough for blacks to hide anywhere."

"Right on!" Jerry Strawberry concurred.

"I agree with Clarkie," said General. "I think it was a hit by the government. This freedom stuff is something that is new to all of us, and they don't want us to take it too far. They want us to remember where we belong. Hey, just look around at this neighborhood! Where are we now?"

"Bobby Kennedy is running for President, once he gets in, we'll be all right," claimed Major.

"Hell, he ain't no more bullet-proof than his brother or King," drawled Jinx.

"You might be right, but I bet he gets some serious protection!" Mo offered.

"How can you get protection against the feds? I bet I live longer than he does and I'm dyin'!" Jinx summed up.

Mary said, "Look fellas, we're not betting that kind of stuff in here. Jinxy, you might be dying, but I don't want to hear that kind of crap in the bar! I go to too many funerals of good people, and God bless you, if I'm still here I'll come to yours, but don't get anybody else involved!"

"I'll drink to that," said Jinx as he pumped down a boilermaker; a shot of whiskey washed down by a frothy Rheingold from the tap. He then took a serious drag on his Marlboro.

In a whisper, Clarkie said to Big Dick, "Man, I'd take that bet, Jinx is killing hisself!"

"You old fool, who's going to pay you?"

While the blood from the assassination of Dr. King tainted the greening of spring, Mo was gaining good jobs in the area as buildings were being removed, and the foundations for new ones were being laid. His bulldozer was a common sight around the rebuilding plots. His constant employment also loosened the tethers that bound him to Mary and the bar.

Chris was in his second year at Howard University, in Washington, D. C. He sported a full-blown Afro and was introduced to the literature of contemporary thought. The struggle of the black experience was bared to him in the *Autobiography of Malcolm X*, and Eldridge Cleaver's *Soul on Ice*, and classics like Booker T. Washington's *Up from Slavery* and W.E.B. DuBois's *Souls of Black Folk* as well as the pre-law courses he was taking. Chris attended anti-war rallies, and raised his clenched fist when greeting other students. He hung out with deposed boxing champ Muhammad Ali, who was a regular speaker at Howard. For the first time in his life, he was concerned with matters that were not played with a ball.

By early June, he was home for the summer vacation. Chris, who could not swim, got a job at a supermarket working in produce. His non-swimming ability preempted any desires to be a lifeguard on the beach.

Chris sat on his bed, as he readied for his first day at his new summer job. His sister Viv's radio was on in her room. She was getting up to go to one of the last days of her school year. The news on the radio entered his room, and he thought he was dreaming. It was about the Kennedy shooting. At thirteen, his sister was not exactly captivated by world events, and having a documentary on about the Kennedy assassination was not her normal fascination, especially at seven in the morning. The more the sound leaked into his room, the more he realized that they were talking about the assassination of Senator Robert Kennedy. "Damn, Bobby got shot, too!" he said to himself. He listened intently as the incredible morning news sifted through the opened door. Chris awoke his seventeen-year-old brother, Stevie, who also had to get up for school.

"Hey man, they shot Kennedy!"

Since Chris had been away at Howard, and Stevie knew of Chris's penchant for being dense at times, figured his brother had not really changed too much and drowsily responded, "Man I know that, November twenty-second, 1963. What are they teaching you at that college?"

"No you doof, they shot Bobby, last night, in L. A.!"

The news of RFK's death astonished America. Martyrs were mounting faster than empty bottles at Joe's Tap on Saturday night. But even more shocking to those at Joe's was the news that Jinx passed, merely two hours *after* the New York senator's murder. During the upsetting day, Joe, Mary, and Mo planned to go to Jinx's funeral, later in the week. Joe decided to close the bar for a couple hours while the service was held. Other regulars sorted through their recollections of Jinx. The television could only speak of Kennedy's death. A common thread of sentiment bouncing around Joe's Tap seemed that if there were saloons in Heaven, Jinx probably found one like Joe's Tap, and was having a good time laughing. For the fast-spreading realization emanating around the bar was that

Jinx would have won his forbidden bet. Word was that Jinx would probably buy the Senator a drink of Irish whiskey when he caught up with him. They all knew that Jinx was gloating over the accuracy of his prediction.

Following Jinx's funeral, there was a ceremony for him that evening in the bar. Joe's Tap "retired" Jinx's barstool. He was enshrined as the first and only member of the Joe's Tap Hall of Fame. A framed, enlarged, picture of Jinx hung over his stool. It was the only photo they could find; Jinx was wearing his Navy uniform, probably more than thirty-five years ago. The tribute was as serious as it could get with the Isley Brothers on the jukebox doing *Twist and Shout*...hey, you can't spell funeral without f-u-n! The Joe's Tap regulars tendered maudlin salutes to Jinx, and wished that he was there to help them "celebrate." Doc had gone to the funeral and offered an articulate tear-filled eulogy. He also praised Jinx in the bar, that evening. Jinx could no longer be a part of this hearty mix. Mary bought a round for the house. Jinx would be missed....

Once the pall of Jinx's death subsided, the regulars got back to business at hand. This was to drink and have fun at each other's expense. As Robert Kennedy's case continued to air on the television and his likely assassin was identified as Sirhan Sirhan, focus in the taproom was directed to Bertha. Although Bertha was likable and buddied with the more outrageous Poison Sumac, she did not escape the attention of the Joe's Tap regulars when they wanted to "roast" someone. Once Bertha returned from her forced hiatus due to her legal problems, the guys took it easy on her. But as time passed, her history became more of a good-natured target. With extended TV time on the accused Kennedy triggerman, the regulars began doubling Bertha's name. She became "Bertha Bertha," the gal who shot her husband.

Robert Kennedy's death, attached to King's, solidified Chris's interest in getting things straightened out. Chris's recently acquired "revolutionary" awareness was given a new platform. He worked his job at the supermarket, read books in his spare time, mostly on history and philosophy, and wrote his girlfriend who lived in Virginia. He was going to be a journalist or an attorney, exposing the conditions of the "disenfranchised" (that was a word he kept seeing in his readings), and get things corrected. This was not the America he wanted to grow old in. Right on, brother!

The losses of Martin Luther King and Robert Kennedy, combined with the pressure mounting over an unpopular war, undermined the patriotic psyche of America. American unity was diffused. Continued misfortunes and psychological depression failed to project Joe's Tap into a position of prominence or even relative fruitfulness. With Jinx gone and all of those social ingredients tumultuously clashing demonically coincided with the onset of Joe's Tap's demise.

Upon the passing of Benito, and with Maurine and Ella finding new homes, another institution of Joe's Tap came to an abrupt end. The chicken coop that had rested in vapid tranquility, next to the earth-moving equipment off and on for twenty-something years was infiltrated by a pillaging vandal--probably a dog; perhaps more than one.

There had never been a foreseen need for reinforcing the coop. It was nothing more than rusted chicken wire nailed to a wood frame of two by fours. It had no lock on its hinged top. There was no Benito to keep order in the backyard. The chicken coop was breached and its occupants were permanently relieved of their egg-laying duties. The sound of the evening music coming from the nearby gazebo band shell possibly masked the cries of the trapped, panicked chickens during their extermination. Mo discovered the aftermath of the attack when he went to warm up his dump truck in the morning. Although three hens survived the massacre, eight productive hens and the rooster were killed. All of this alerted Joe and Mary that they were vulnerable to other calamities if they did not get a better handle on things inside the bar, as well. The war and assassinations were not stellar moments for America; the destroyed chickens were a gloomy preamble for the systematic collapse of Joe's Tap.

Chapter Fourteen *Oh Canada!*

J oe and Mary began to feel the pinch of a decreasing customer base, and tried to devise innovative concepts to stay up with the turbulent times. An unavoidable problem, which they faced and could do nothing about, was they were getting older. Their business ideas were not necessarily marching in step into the 1970s. A more shocking punch to the solar plexus was that a failing neighborhood bar had recently been sold and relocated down the street with a new name, and courted black business.

The other bar had paralleled Joe's Tap's existence. With essentially aging white clientele, it had been owned by a Jewish family and stood on the perimeter of the rebuilding neighborhood, closer to the beach. It had also been marked for removal. Its liquor license sold, and a new site was secured that travelers into town would strategically pass before they got to Joe's Tap. The fresh image of Sterling's Silver Slipper Lounge's theme and focus was on a younger crowd. It did not contain the Depression and World War II era drivel from guys born in the aughts and teens that prevailed as a staple at Joe's. It had six color TVs and played hipper music. Also, the owner, Sterling, was black, a retired local policeman, and had yet to pull a gun on anyone--even as a cop!

Feeling the singes of competition's heat, Joe and Mary plotted their first significant remodel of Joe's Tap since they bought it. Fresh paint, a color TV, and some new stools and tables temporarily rescued the bar from its withdrawal into a state of all-purpose dinginess.

The Vietnam War destabilized American patriotism that had not been this challenged since the Civil War. Young men were forced to make a decision about fighting a battle on the other side of the globe. America's involvement in Vietnam was something no one could clearly explain to them (the Domino Theory, perhaps?) why. The real possibility of coming home in a coffin, whence some officer handed their bereaved mother a folded American flag, or getting out of the country seemed like the only choices. A favorite bumper sticker of the day, "America: Love It, or Leave It!" gave few middle-ground solutions, and some thought that to stay was to die.

As a subliminal diversion from the Vietnam War and another jab at supremacy in the Cold War, the United States became the first country to send a man to the moon. In 1969, Neil Armstrong became the first human to set foot on Earth's distant satellite. Reaching the moon did not bring world peace or an ending to the Vietnam War. It was good theater at a time when patriotism vacillated.

Antonio had chosen to enlist in the Navy in 1966. He was nowhere close to graduating from high school. The path of life that he navigated was not always in his own best interest. He had a police record for a litany of misdemeanors. It was just a matter of time before he got arrested for a felony or did something for which to get shot. Some of his friends were doing time, and most of them had done drugs. Small-town Cape May could not avoid the wave of narcotics cascading across the country.

Antonio knew that he would be drafted immediately after walking away from school for the last time. He opted for the Navy because like many people associated with Cape May, he liked boats, and someone told him that North Vietnam did not have a navy. He liked those odds. But a funny thing happened on his way to becoming a commodore; he was not sworn into the Navy, because he had traces of cocaine in his system during a pre-induction physical examination. The Navy told him to come back when he got cleaned up. He turned to the Marines and they promptly accepted him. He used his background growing up in a bar, in addition to a lot of luck, and became a bartender in the officer's club; first, south of Saigon, and then in Hawaii. He never witnessed combat; he never really had to carry a weapon. Honorably discharged from the Marines, he was a legitimate veteran of the Vietnam War. With a more mature bearing, he had an opportunity to re-vamp a business in a re-developing town. Antonio had emerged as the titular heir apparent, while he tended bar, at Joe's Tap.

As a bartender, Antonio was not hard to find. His days of milling around Cape May with his directionless friends were not that long ago. One thing that he brought with him from the service was a sense of honor and loyalty. This matter of loyalty was not so much for the military, but for his friends and family. He neither sought fighting in a rice field nor did he run from it. He was never ordered into combat, and he did not jump at the front of the line to be there. He dutifully did what he was told.

One balmy late summer afternoon while Antonio was working in the bar, a former childhood beach buddy came in looking for him. It was the second such visit from the friend who was on leave from the Army. His friend was now on an "extended" leave from his infantry unit. He was supposed to have shipped out on his way to Vietnam four days before. The authorities were looking for him and they had already been to his home a couple of times. He figured that he was just a step ahead of the Military Police, for they were interviewing his friends as well as other family members. In short order, he expected they would be quizzing Antonio. He was hoping, and expecting, that he could rely on Antonio.

Antonio's friend, Jimmy Bowersox was absent without leave, AWOL. Antonio told him that he could crash upstairs in Ella's old room. He advised Mary, who was sitting with Mo in the bar, that he had invited his friend to stay for a couple of days. They all knew Jimmy and his family, and everything was fine. Joe was at the other end talking to Major and Big Dick. Everything was fine for all of three hours when two stern-faced, uniformed MPs entered the bar carrying an official paper in hand.

One MP was black the other was white. Jimmy was white, which allowed him to stand out with conspicuous prominence among the black customers of Joe's Tap, if he was still in the bar. Jimmy, who was upstairs and tired from his dodging the government, had quickly drifted off to sleep. The MPs advanced toward Antonio, and asked for the owner, and he sent them to Joe. They go down to the end of the bar where Joe is sipping a beer with the regulars. Antonio casually went over to Mo and asked him to find a good spot to hide Jimmy, while he anticipated that he was surely on the MPs' agenda.

By now the MPs were talking to Joe, and trying to find out if Jimmy had been around. Joe said, "I haven't seen that boy for a couple of years. Hell, I haven't seen much of anything for a couple of years! You ought to talk to my wife. No, talk to my nephew about Jimmy, he's the bartender. But if you have anything to read, show Mary." Joe nodded in the direction where Mary was sitting. The MP walked over to Mary and presented a document to allow them to look throughout the premises. Mary lifted her suspended reading glasses from in front of her chest to the bridge of her nose and scanned the paper. She consented.

The soldiers re-approached Antonio. The white MP sat across the bar from him; the black MP stood behind the seated MP. He scrutinized the bar and tables. They both presented an official and devout exterior.

Antonio whose hair was modishly long asked, "Fellows, what'll you have?"

The white MP asked, "Are you Antonio Salerno?"

"That's right. Guys, I have served in Vietnam, and I am not looking to go back, if you're recruiting!" Antonio is putting on his best bartender face. He sets a coaster, with Benito's likeness on it, in prelude to the soldier's bar order, which is not forthcoming.

"We are looking for Private James Bowersox and we heard that you might know where he is," the MP said.

The black MP strolled around the bar, getting ogled from Poison Sumac and Bertha Bertha, who are tipsy and silly.

"Hey soldier, you gotta place to stay tonight?" blurted Poison Sumac playfully.

He does not reply; it is all business for him. He is in his early twenties; with a buffed body stretching his sharply creased khaki uniform. He wore a shiny black helmet with "MP" on the front of it. "My husband can sleep on the porch," she continued.

"Honey, that boy is about the same age as your David. You oughta quit being so fresh!" Bertha Bertha admonished.

"Look, I nursed David for a year and a half; I sure wouldn't mind nursing 'General Blackstud' over there for an hour and a half!" The women slapped each other five, and laughed at the far-flung scenario. They tipped their glasses at the MP and had another drink.

"Sergeant, he was in here a couple weeks ago, but he was shipping out. We went to Wildwood last week and did some drinking for his send-off. But that is as much as I know," Antonio told the white MP.

Upstairs, Mo got angular Jimmy up from his rest and grabbed the military duffle bag Jimmy came in with. He rushed him down the steps opposite from where the soldiers patrolled. He led him into the pantry. This was the same pantry where Joe assaulted Ella four summers before. Mo put Jimmy in the corner of a walk-in cooler behind cases of beer that were in the pantry. He quickly built some empty boxes onto the full ones, in an impromptu camouflage maneuver.

"You stay here until I come and get you," Mo firmly told Jimmy, and turned the light out. Mo proudly served in World War II, but understood the moral strain this war was having on people. He had known Jimmy for years. Jimmy chilled in the cooler and promptly began to shiver from the temperature and his fear of being detected. Mo slowly paced toward the bar. The black MP probed his way toward the pantry, and bumped into Mo who was in waiting.

Mo said, "Where the hell you goin'?"

"Sir, I have permission from Mrs. Di Cicco to come back here," replied the soldier.

"Oh, I am Mo, maybe I can help you, and I work here. I just don't want nobody sneaking back here and taking something, ya know! What do you need? I've been here for twenty years. I know where everything is."

"Sir, Private James Bowersox is absent without leave, and we have to take him with us."

"Well, unless Jimmy is shaped like a bottle of Crown Royal and hiding in a purple pouch, or wearing a mouse outfit, he ain't back there. You can look if you want!"

"Thank you, sir!" The MP took a step toward the pantry; an ominous step toward uncovering a quivering, cowering, hiding Jimmy.

Just then, a well-fed rat scampered along a nearby wall and startled the MP. The intensity with which he came into the pantry area trembled him a bit, and he said to Mo, "Sir, no one is back there, correct?"

"Hell no, not on my watch! That is my job to make sure things are tight. I live here; I don't want nobody sneaking in on me. Just don't tell the health department about that mouse!" The MP worked a humor-prompted grunt at Mo's understatement of the rodent's stature.

"We used to have a bad-assed dog that took care of those freaking rodents, but he is gone now. That was a hell of a dog!" Mo's charm was disarming and convincing. Talking his way out of jams was nothing new to him. Mo had been in the service and knew that he and Joe's Tap were committing a potential felony, jeopardizing their liquor license, and worse. Mo continued on to the bar and the MP followed him. After about ten minutes of ducking into rooms and peeking in closets, the soldiers departed Joe's Tap. Mo watched them get into a military car in the parking lot across the street, and they drove off. He walked outside and made sure they kept on going.

Not wanting to get busted for "harboring a fugitive," Mo hurried into the pantry and gathered Jimmy from behind the boxes, which probably would not have provided thorough enough cover for Jimmy if the MP was purposeful in doing his job. Jimmy shivered like a plucked banjo string. Mo told Antonio to make Jimmy a sandwich, get him a boiled egg, and a bottled Pepsi. He got the keys from Mary to her Cadillac. Mo only had a front-end loader available, which would not be an ideal getaway vehicle. Jimmy began to eat his meal out of sight from the bar as Mo went to the car and made sure the trunk was empty. Mo rushed Jimmy to the side door of the bar and looked up and down the intersection. Seeing the coast was clear he put Jimmy in the trunk, partial sandwich, soda, and all. Mo made sure that Jimmy had money, of which Jimmy was OK, and drove him out of Cape May to Wildwood to catch the bus to Atlantic City, on its way to making connections to Toronto, Ontario, Canada. Jimmy was curled in the sweltering trunk just moments removed from crouching in the cooler of Joe's Tap. In Wildwood, Mo went into the bus station and purchased the ticket to Atlantic City for Jimmy. Mo made sure he exited the trunk out of sight from any meddling eyes, and saw him onto the bus. No one heard from Jimmy for a long time.

The corporate fate of Joe's Tap rested largely in the hands of Antonio. Mary and Joe had been in the same spot for almost twenty-five years. Joe's eyesight was all but a memory. Mary was a grouchy, middle-aged woman, and a burden to be around for either Joe or Mo. The work she had delegated in the past to Ella and Maurine was not getting done. If she hired someone to do it, she would invariably scare them away with her acerbic, almost belligerent directions. Slaves were in short supply in 1970. Jerry Strawberry fit in well and got along with Joe, Mary, Mo, and Antonio, because he worked hard and did not care to go back to North Carolina and work dawn to dusk in a tobacco field.

Carmen left the bar one mid-summer night with a customer, and did not reappear for two weeks. Mary had Carmen's things boxed up waiting for her when she returned, and gave her until noon the next day to get out. Carmen had paid minimal rent, and took huge liberties with Mary and Joe for over twenty years. She chose to have little input when Antonio and Ella were growing up. Aside from showing up, almost as often as Halley's Comet on her scheduled times in the bar, she made herself expendable. Sadly, Mary had no one else who was any more reliable. Mary was simply not in the frame of mind to tolerate Carmen's juvenile-like complacency. However, it was not difficult for Carmen to find a place to stay, and she left. She was 50 at the time. Over the years, Carmen and Mary remained close as sisters, but shared no business association.

Jerry Strawberry and Antonio evolved into a seventies version of Mo and Joe. They worked together and drank together, and more. While Mary was a constant thorn in the side for both of them, the bar stayed floating above the red ink. However, Mary could not curtail their penchant for using drugs. In ensuing months that became a critical problem for Joe's Tap, and Mary had no answers.

Jerry Strawberry talked in the vernacular of the rural South. He was a product of an extended family that share cropped tobacco, corn, and pigs, and would be just as happy if he never revisited that portion of his life. His family had resided in the same area for generations. There were entries in the family Bible of births going back to the 1840s. It was not known who made those entries because Jerry Strawberry and his siblings and cousins were the first generation of that family to read and write. His family lived the dawn-to-dusk work schedule, in a brutally repressive racial environment. Jerry Strawberry was born with a colorful name. With his reddish-dyed processed hair, sometimes-peculiar facial tics, and oddball way of speaking, was eventually nicknamed "Agent Orange."

Agent Orange was the defoliant the American military had used to clear leaves from trees and bushes to better isolate enemies in hiding in Vietnam jungles. In the early 1970s Doc read that research into Agent Orange showed an unhealthy consequence, physically and mentally on people, including American troops, and shared this with the less-read bar regulars. Jerry Strawberry was not wounded in the war by bombs or bullets, but his personality was obviously different from what it had been prior to his term in the Army. It was even different from when he hired on at Joe's Tap. Jerry Strawberry was Agent Orange!

Chapter Fifteen *Darrin*

After almost three years, Maurine was still living with Adele in Philadelphia. Things had not gone the way she envisioned. She dropped out of the College of Art the year before. She told Mo that the program was not what she was expecting. The emphasis was more commercially oriented which did not feed into her desire to be creatively free. That was partially true. She could have easily transferred her credits and moved into that phase of the curriculum. In fact, she became pregnant and had a child. She quit school to be a single mother. There was a swath of time that she could not work, and in those pressurized moments Adele badgered her about money. When she wasn't railing about rent she was agitated with the baby crying.

For about three months, Maurine was locked in a torment from which there was no escape. Although it was not the case, Adele essentially accused Maurine of having sex with one of her boyfriends that caused her maternity. Adele's intemperate insecurity jiggled that cage's door. However, the real sting was that the father was the manager of the doughnut shop where Maurine had been employed. He was also married, and had no intention of revising that situation. Maurine had developed some specific goals for herself. Her underlying motivation was to not wake up one day and be besieged with the malingering traits of the people she viewed at Joe's Tap. She now imagined one foot sliding into that trap, and the other one in a reality that she might already be snared.

She had not planned on having a child, especially with no father in the picture. She stopped beating herself up about how this came about, for there was no acceptable explanation. Things happen! She was lonely, curious, and away from Joe's Tap. And the guy sniffed around her with enchanting and relentless blandishment from the day he hired her. Knowing that Adele would be at work late on a drab afternoon, she invited him over on a day she felt particularly down. He failed to mention that he had a wife until she told him of her pregnancy. She undertook responsibility herself, and paid the demanding hospital bill.

Maurine transitioned into working full time at a large department store in Philadelphia, as a sales clerk in the women's clothing section. She had a natural capacity to connect with customers, and in a short time was recognized by her bosses and fellow workers for her savvy and sales instinct. With the help of the maximum earnings she could achieve through her quarterly bonus, she was making just enough to exist comfortably in poverty.

When the baby boy got older, she planned on going to the community college if she could just not be undone by Adele's quirky rants. A large portion of her pay went to satisfy rent--current and past. What little remained, went to a babysitter, diapers, and baby food. The father was no help. She sought not to expose the man as the father of her child, plus he already had two kids with his wife. She had very little money left for any fun. Life was not fun, except for playing with her son, Darrin.

Darrin was a delightful spark of motivation for Maurine. None of this was what Maurine had seen in her personal crystal ball, but this was her life and Darrin's life. She would deal with it. However, she was going to give Darrin all the mothering that she could never find during her own youth. She would give him the fathering, as best that she could, when it was called for. Darrin responded to her affectionate doting by his incessant grinning.

On a Wednesday morning, Maurine prepared for work. She got herself dressed, and went over to Darrin's crib to get him ready for the babysitter. Usually, Darrin would be crawling around waiting for her, anticipating a morning gambol with Maurine and his bottle.

Maurine went to get him and immediately recognized that Darrin was not moving in his customary fashion. She picked him up and there was no response. She shook him and there was still nothing. She screamed for Adele who was sound asleep. Adele arrived in ill-humor until she realized the severity of the situation. Darrin was inconceivably lifeless.

Adele called for the paramedics and within five minutes they were in the apartment. They tried to resuscitate Darrin, to no avail. They rushed him to the ambulance, hooked to machines, and sped off to the children's hospital. A befuddled and distraught Maurine went with him. Darrin had yet to move.

Within an hour of arrival, the emergency room doctor told Maurine that Darrin had died during the night. There were no marks of abuse or an accident. It was possibly a case of sudden infant death syndrome, but the death would have to be investigated. For Maurine, none of this mattered. The how and why would just accentuate the truth. Darrin was dead, and nothing could justify that.

Adele arrived. She consoled Maurine as well as she could, and tried to take her back to the apartment. Maurine was inconsolable, and did not want to leave without Darrin.

Mary required Maurine and Ella, with almost with ghoulish preponderance, to attend funerals as youngsters. Maurine usually had but a passing knowledge of the departed, who were either bar patrons or members of the church. Those experiences were never exhilarating. Only once was it for a child; the fourteen-year-old boy from her and Ella's Sunday school class. Never was it for a baby. Now she must find the resolve and fortitude to face burying seven-month-old Darrin Garnet Finch, her son.

Maurine qualified for life insurance at work and was covered for Darrin. There was enough money for a funeral, and a small cemetery marker. The days leading up to the service glided along for Maurine in a surreal, cinematic, slow motion blur. Nothing made sense. There was no plausible way for Maurine to comprehend the death of Darrin. The following Monday morning, Darrin's funeral was scheduled. Adele was respectfully censured from telling anyone in Cape May what had happened by the grieving Maurine. She also posed the same request at the baby's birth. As much as she knew,

Adele honored those requests. Maurine continued to maintain her distance from Mo.

The service was small, at Adele's church, with her minister conducting. A few of Maurine's co-workers came to support her at this dreadful time. Adele was there and sang a religious tribute to Darrin. Her voice was comforting and stimulating; it was an uplifting contribution. Adele's talent had been repressed by her own blunders in life, but she had the ability to find the right tone for this service. Maurine, despite the petty feuds that she and Adele shared over the years, found inspirational strength in Adele's vocal interpretation and her depth of feeling. She thanked her with a hug as they went to the cemetery. The funeral staff served as pallbearers and carried the miniature coffin.

Maurine had never felt overwhelming grief before. She had probably been to 15 funerals, and was deeply saddened by each of them. For her, Benito's passing was as shocking a loss as anything up to now. There was absolutely nothing to come close to the incomprehensible and heart-breaking death of Darrin. But really, at day's end what was left in Philly for her? Nothing that she could see was convincing enough to keep her there. Where now? Cape Island? Devil's Island had more allure. She could not return home. That was not an option. She certainly could not return home as a self-proclaimed failure, which this episode in her life was making her feel like. Darrin's death as horrible as it was would not be as abysmal as returning to Cape May and Joe's Tap. She needed some time to think. She needed to sort out her life.

Chapter Sixteen *the Attic*

M aurine took a couple days off from work. She was allowed the time off. She needed to work but was not in the emotional state to deal with the acknowledgments of sympathy, or people clumsily avoiding her for the want of knowing what to say. She decided to get on the trolley and go to the main library. She could hide away in the books and stacks and read and research anything that moved her. This would be her emotional therapy, and maybe along the way she might just learn something.

She demurred on going back to the art college and she was not thrilled working her job just to pay rent at Adele's and having life insurance protection and a pension. She would browse magazines and atlases to see if there was any place on Earth she wanted to be that wasn't named Cape May or Philadelphia. As those couple of secluded days passed, the one place on Earth that she could get to, and had an appealing ring to it, was on the bay on the opposite side of the country. In 1970, the foremost area in America in this time of personal expression seemed to be San Francisco, California.

She worked on Thursday and Friday. She called her aunt to see if she could stay for the weekend in West Cape May. Her aunt was happy to hear from her, and agreed. She suspected that Adele, her Aunt Rachel's daughter, might have filled her in about her life in Philadelphia, but little of her past was worth the effort to cover up. Whatever!

On Friday afternoon she left work two hours early and boarded the train to Cape May; the same train she would greet as a five-year-old, seeking her mother. She tried to anticipate her reception upon her arrival but there was little to excite her about her return. Right on schedule, the train arrived at six-fifteen. Maurine walked the few steps to Joe's Tap. Antonio and Mary were in the bar. Antonio was elated to see her. Mary smiled but was not doing somersaults upon her entrance.

Little had changed since she left Joe's Tap. She looked around the bar and things were in the same spot they had always been. She noticed the new tables and chairs. She glanced at the color TV. She wasn't sure for what she was expecting. But she was back in Joe's Tap.

"Little Mo, girl how are you?" Antonio hollered. "You are looking damn good!"

"I'm OK. I'm glad to see you are not in some long-term penal institution," she said jokingly.

"Oh, and this isn't?"

"Hey kid, looking for a job?" Mary asked dispassionately.

"Could be, but not here!" Maurine responded with an equally straight face. "Is Daddy around?"

"He was here a moment ago, he's probably in his room," Mary answered.

"I'll be back in a few." Maurine detoured to the side porch where Joe and three of his racing buddies were tallying their latest losses, looking for their big score.

"Hey Uncle Joe, how are you? Hey guys!" Maurine was wary of Joe and now believed him to be the father of Ella's son. However, she did not have the same negative karma about him as with Mary or her father. They got along.

"Maurine, is that you? Glad to have you back. You staying for a while?" Joe was cordial and refreshingly sincere. She could see he was aging and not so gracefully. The mustache was gone and replaced with unattended gray stubble all over his face. His once neat black hair was gloomily gray and shaggy with overgrown sideburns. His once brown eyes were as gray as his hair and focused on nothing. He talked in the general direction of the person with whom he was in conversation. He had lost the vitality of the guy who ran a bar and broke up fights, for the last twenty-five years; the hard-nosed Joe she remembered.

"I am just visiting, and I wanted to say hello."

"OK dear, don't stay away so long!"

Maurine reentered the bar and Joe put the radio back to his ear. She proceeded to the steps just as Mo is coming down them. She waited at the bottom as Mo saw her.

"Hello Daddy!"

"Hey Baby! What, you need a loan?" Mo said. He hit the floor the same time as his cynicism and caution did. Mo looked pretty much as she recalled from the last time, when he took her to college. Maurine embraced Mo. Mo was not quite sure what to do. Neither of them remembered the last time they hugged, prompting Mo to mindlessly say, "You got big!" Maurine needed to hug her father because despite their somewhat estranged relationship, he was always "Daddy" and the only real family that she knew. The hug also aided in what was about to transpire next.

"Yes, I do need some money, enough to get me back into the art college. I don't want to squander the rest of my life working in a department store because I ran out of money!"

"Hmm, how much are we talking about?" Mo's demeanor was far more subdued than when he tended bar.

"I need a thousand dollars by Monday!"

"You staying with Aunt Rachel?"

"Yes, for tonight and tomorrow. Can you help me?"

"Look for me tomorrow in the bar, I'll be around." Mo walked toward the bar, apparently not looking to extend his surprise reunion with Maurine any longer.

"Thanks, I am going to say good-bye to everybody and walk to Aunt Rachel's."

Maurine decided to go up the stairs into the attic before she went off to Aunt Rachel's. Upon her entrance, it looked like it always did, erratically cluttered. She and Ella were the only ones to frequent the attic and would store bar items there. Most of the stuff was still where they put it, as long as fifteen years ago. However, what she was looking for most was not there. She could not locate the records that Elmo had given her over the years. She had them organized and cataloged. She had left them in eleven standard-sized plastic milk cartons. Many of them were slotted in albums she had purchased. Thus among the chaotic mess of the attic, her records would stick out like snowflakes in the Sahara. She could especially not see the hi-fi set that she bought in the eighth grade. She frantically moved and lifted crates, boxes, and stored bar equipment in search of her delicate treasure. Her search did not go well. Johnny Mathis had been abducted.

Today was not a good time for bad news. After proving to her ultimate dissatisfaction that the records were missing, she cried. She sat on a box and sobbed. She buried her son on Monday, and on Friday the only thing about Joe's Tap, for her, that she could put a happy face on, was the almost one thousand records Elmo had given her. Those classics spanned over a decade of popular culture, and in a weird way provided a mystical bond with her still faceless mother. She sat and stewed in her own hushed melancholy for an hour while the sunlight in the dusty room faded to complete darkness.

Maurine finally composed herself. She did not want to confront Mary about the records. Whatever Mary said was going to anger her possibly to the point of Maurine wanting to physically harm her. Maurine deduced that she owed Mary an ass-whipping for a plethora of serious slights, but not today. She knew her father would side with Mary, and that would compound the fracture. For the moment, she needed her father. The way she felt reminded her why she left Joe's Tap to begin with. This was as good as Mary would ever let her feel. She needed the twenty minute walk to West Cape May. She would come back to Joe's Tap tomorrow, and see what her father would do. She couldn't carry the records anywhere if she had them, but he should have consulted her about any sale; they were hers!

On Saturday afternoon, while making some rounds seeing Ella and her four-year-old son Jason, and former neighborhood acquaintances, she passed Stevie Mitchell who was riding a bicycle to work at the tennis courts. Maurine and Stevie had not been particularly close, but they knew each other casually, especially during the time when his brother, Chris, was enamored with Maurine.

Stevie was about to start his second year at Rutgers University. He directed his studies toward political science, perhaps with an eye on going into law. They caught up on each other's recent lives, and of course the topic became what Chris was doing.

"Chris just graduated from Howard. My Mom, my sister, and I went to the ceremony. Caught the train right next to Joe's Tap, you know!" Stevie told Maurine.

"So did he get a job yet?"

"Yeah, he's working. He's training to be a retail manager. I thought that he was going into law, or get an MBA, maybe; I can't believe it! He's getting paid pretty well, but the job is in Virginia somewhere. That's where his fiancée lives. He announced he's getting married next June."

"Fiancée, wow!" Maurine felt her knees quiver.

Plied with Darrin's death, and her missing phonograph records, Chris's impending marriage was an additional jolt of depressing news. She had neither forgotten him, nor the great talks that they shared. Something about Chris and her just seemed to click on the highest plane. "The next time you talk to him, mention that I ask for him and I truly wish him well."

"Right on, I have to get to work!" Stevie departed, leaving an emotionally susceptible Maurine deflated by Chris's apparent happiness and imminent betrothal.

Maurine returned to Joe's Tap to see what her father was going to offer, if anything. Maurine's last birthday was her twenty-first, and she sat at the bar as a legitimate paying customer for the first time.

Antonio said, "Little Mo, you drinking now?"

As much as anything, Maurine just wanted to see what it was like to order a drink from Joe's Tap. Perhaps it was to get a feel for what all of those people, during her time there, felt when she watched them lose the better part of their sobriety and corresponding decorum.

"I'll have a Long Island tea," Maurine responded.

"Darn, you hang with the big girls, now!"

"Maybe I am a big girl!"

"Keep your money Little Mo, it's on me."

"Thanks Antonio, I appreciate that."

Maurine sat and sipped while waiting for Mo. By the time she got half-way through the mixed drink, she sensed the bar begin to spin around. Her feeling was like being in recess on the playground, and whirling around a bunch of times and then coming to a stop. Mo entered and sat next to her while she was finding that she wanted to giggle at everything, even while clinging to the memory of Darrin.

"Hello Daddy," she grinned. She knew that the alcohol teased her, but she did not want that to blatantly evidence itself while she was talking to Mo. Ironically, Mo was a professional bartender and knew a drunk when he saw one. Mo noticed Maurine's diminished sobriety.

"Look, this is the best I can do, and don't blow it all here at the bar!" There was no fanfare or expression of joy in his voice; just limited fatherly advice. Maurine, in her light-headed state, suspected this was her father's payoff; the *bon voyage* that he did not offer when she went off to college.

Mo also knew of the birth and death of the child, his grandson. Adele was not one to keep secrets very well, especially when rent was past due. Mo felt for Maurine and disapproved that she did not tell him about Darrin. However, he was neither going to apologize for the life he lived, nor did he expect Maurine to apologize for hers. She was certainly a creation of the situation in which he raised her. Maurine had moved from Joe's Tap while in high school and she did not allow Mo to have an audience with his grandson. Both Mo and Maurine provided the other with enough mounting personal baggage that could doom their progressively tenuous relationship.

Maurine looked at the money in her hand, and counted six-one hundred dollar bills.

"Thank you, I'll do right by this," she vowed. "Oh and Daddy, do you know where my records and record player are? I looked in the attic yesterday and did not see them."

"I just handed them to you. A guy made an offer in the bar, a collector. Six hundred dollars; Antonio has the record player. Who knew you was coming back?"

Maurine pondered what her father said. She tried to figure out how anyone knew to ask about the record collection. "Daddy, was it you or Mary who sold them?"

"Actually, I was going to give you the grand, but I took out four-hundred bucks for the booze you stole. Take the money!" He said nothing more. Mo got up and headed back to his room. Maurine interpreted his overall reticence to mean that Mary probably instigated the record sale, but he probably helped. She also suspected they probably got more than a thousand dollars. At least this is the way they used to do things; Mary would think stuff up, and Mo would do the heavy lifting.

Maurine finished her drink and ordered another one. She looked into the mirror behind the bar. She saw the reflection of the people she watched as a child. The ones who measured the depth of their problems by the number of drinks they consumed. She shockingly realized it's her own face. No, it can't be!

While finishing her drink, her inebriated mind wandered to an area that she had not visited for a while. Maurine envisioned herself crashing Chris's wedding wearing a wedding dress. She was living the Benjamin role from *the Graduate*.

"Chris!" She hollered through the closed church door in her daydream.

"Maurine!" Upon yelling her name, Chris took a step back to look for her.

"Chris!" With that Chris responded by leaving his bride at the altar to find Maurine.

He and Maurine united and barricaded the church door as they ran off. The entire church congregation broke through the door and chased after them. They hopped on the train next to Joe's Tap. The train did not go anywhere and Chris was retrieved by his bride and taken back to conclude his wedding. Maurine sat on the train in the white wedding dress with Mary sitting on her restricting her from going after Chris.

Maurine regained her senses and came back to reality. She finally got up from her stool and bade good-bye to Antonio. She waved to Mary on one end of the bar and walked to the opposite end and kissed Joe good-bye. She passed folks who had not seen her in a long while. It was almost five years since she last worked around the bar. She was happy to see everyone, but just as happy to be walking out the door before she could not. She had seen it too many times; people who got trapped in a bottle and could not get out. She was going out standing, with no intention of returning.

On an overcast Sunday morning, while waiting to catch the train back to Philadelphia, Maurine took a look at Joe's Tap. It never occurred to her that would be the last glance at her home. She went to the intersection and looked down the street to see the ocean on the horizon. She savored the salted breeze. The clean air allayed the bubbling stomach she had from last night's drinks, her personal mourning, and the nervousness of her troubling internalized decisions. She even gave thought to Chris, a source of personal happiness during a special time in her life, and the prospect of him being married. Why would he enter into her thoughts so often? She had not even seen him in five years! The train's whistle blared; she got aboard, headed for her uncharted future.

On Monday morning, she went to work and resigned her position. She instructed them to have her pay sent to an address when she got one. She would call them with that information. Maurine would be on the 6:05 p.m. plane soaring for San Francisco with the money her father gave her to resume college. It was to be a non-stop, one-way excursion into destiny. The thought that she knew no one there was less daunting than the people that she did know on the East Coast. Going out there with no job was far less constricting than staying in Philadelphia. However, this had to happen now, before something came up that would not let her leave. Maurine was gone!

Chapter Seventeen *West Coast*

Maurine did not take long to acclimate to San Francisco. She scarcely missed the Haight-Ashbury, "hippy" movement. She hung out with diverse personalities that she could never fantasize about in Cape May or even Philadelphia. She landed a job working for the telephone utility in San Francisco. She was punctual and reliable. She enrolled in community college on a part-time basis taking art classes. Maurine still sported the natural hair, and had slimmed to her pre-maternity weight of around 150 pounds. She was now an incredibly good looking 22-year-old woman.

Maurine's real personality showed for probably the first time in her life. She was in a community of little pretense and she had to answer to no one outside of work. Everyone seemed to have his or her own sphere of orbit, and it was accepted without judgment or critique. From her small apartment she was a caring and social neighbor. She was invited into people's homes, and she hosted her new acquaintances. She frequented the neighborhood night spots. The characters at these stops were often as varied as the mode of dress that adorned them.

She flourished in the section of San Francisco known as the Western Addition. It was 3000 miles from Cape May in more than just distance. The Western Addition, which bordered the Fillmore District, was the polar opposite of Cape May.

Once the Japanese were relocated following the bombing of Pearl Harbor, African-Americans moved into those vacated homes. Following World War II, these parts of San Francisco became ethnically diverse and prospered in its burgeoning multiplicity.

When the Japanese returned following the war, they contributed to the area's positive growth. It was probably the first San Francisco district to fully embrace African-Americans.

Jewish, Asian and African-American neighborhoods mixed easily in this community. During its period of urban renewal, old Victorian houses were torn down for modern houses and apartments to absorb the demand of people wanting to live there. It was rebuilt and re-energized, and became a great place to call home and simultaneously be a tourist destination. When the fog was not thick, and from her apartment on a hill, Maurine could view the Golden Gate Bridge; Alcatraz sat in the bay.

Maurine attended parties that had students, lesbians, pimps, corporate attorneys, street walkers, hustlers, professors, homosexuals, ordained ministers, cross-dressers, and school teachers. Every conceivable ethnic community was a part of her existence. There was hardly a segment of American life that she did not encounter. After perfunctory drug experimentation, she sought not to further visit that villain. She could witness the damage drugs did to the ones she cared about in her coterie of friends, and the ones who were not. At Joe's Tap, she had witnessed similar ravages of dissolution brought on by alcohol abuse. She could never understand why those people would torture themselves and the people in their lives like that. In Western Addition, there were many chances to lend an ear and offer an encouraging hug.

In 1974, she encountered a young man on the fast track, and he readily moved in with her. This guy was a third year law student at Cal-Berkeley. Her boyfriend, Jonas Henry had been a NCAA 400 meter hurdles finalist, and just missed going to the Munich Olympics in 1972. He had completed his undergraduate degree at San Jose State University. Jonas enjoyed handsome light-skinned features, good grades, a quick wit, and a stellar future.

Jonas met Maurine at a party. They both were conspicuous because they were virtually the only ones there without a garishly attired agenda. For the rest of the world, they probably looked like "regular people." In the bohemian world that was San Francisco, they were boldly an "anachronism." Their dress was a throwback to a time of convention.

Maurine was comfortable with Jonas. For the first time in her life she availed herself to a man without the threat of anyone looking over her shoulder. She exorcised every Catholic school demon in her sexual expression with Jonas. At twenty-five, Maurine sensed her life was beginning to come together as she imagined in her Johnny Mathis records.

Jonas was about to graduate from law school in December 1975. He had interviewed and garnered solid offers from a number of firms, nationally. He was black, articulate, and marketable. He chose a firm in Atlanta, Georgia, with a high profile reputation in civil rights cases. Jonas asked Maurine to come with him. He did not ask her to marry him. She decided, after missing him for about three weeks, to make the move. Maurine completed her courses, quit her job with the telephone company, and followed Jonas to Atlanta.

The city and the apartment were spectacular, but Maurine's verve did not gel with her new situation. In a short time, she realized that Jonas's associates had the pretense that she did not find in San Francisco. The fact that she barely had more than a high school education proved a burden that undermined her empathy for Atlanta, and ultimately her relationship with Jonas. Any disparity in education was not an issue while in California. Atlanta was like sucking Jell-O through a straw; she could do it, but was tired and unfulfilled from the effort. Maurine found the heat and the people oppressive. Southern hospitality proved too cliquish. She missed Western Addition, but had no job or a place to live back there. Still, she had to get out of Atlanta.

Maurine saw a classified advertisement in the *Atlanta Constitution* for "women territorial marketing managers" with British-based *Penthouse* magazine. She bought a *Penthouse* to get a flavor for its content. Having lived in San Francisco offered her a value system that went far beyond the suppressed way she was brought up in Cape May. She applied for a position and was given an interview in Atlanta. Whether it was the need to find a job that was far removed from her Catholic school regimen and to assert her individuality, or just get a job, it didn't much matter; she wanted to move on.

Although Maurine was now fully initiated into sex, she did not want to be a naked exhibit in the magazine, and easily could have been. She charged full speed ahead to win one of those marketing jobs. Maurine had earned an associate's degree, where the ad requested college grads. When Maurine got dressed to impress, she looked like success. Her experience working in the department store honed her perspective on the influence of clothing. In her preliminary interview in Atlanta, there were two people who screened candidates; a man and a woman. She did not know how many people nationally or in Atlanta were being considered, but two days later she got the call from the woman who told her that *Penthouse* wanted to further interview her. They requested for her to come to New York for domestic corporate interviews and an orientation period, if all went well. They gave her a round-trip plane ticket, accommodations in a "basic" Manhattan hotel in the theater district on Broadway. Meal money and cab fare made her feel "rich." She had never been to New York, even though it was three hours from Cape May.

Maurine dazzled in her interviews and orientation. She declined the inevitable invitation to pose in the magazine. Some seeds were never meant to grow. She only came for the territorial job, and that is what she went back to Atlanta holding. After three days, she flew back to Atlanta to get her belongings. Jonas, who worked constantly, was aware of Maurine's discomfort, and gave a sincere effort to show support. He tried his best summation (much of it sexual) to convince her to remain in his life, but the jury did not take long for its verdict. Maurine left Jonas and Atlanta.

After originally being told that she was going to Vancouver, British Columbia, Maurine was ordered to Pittsburgh, Pennsylvania. She operated a territory in western Pennsylvania, the panhandle of West Virginia, and eastern Ohio which included Cleveland and Columbus. She had a company car, salary and bonuses, and an expense account. She was also consistently alone.

Maurine's dynamic was a perfect fit for her job. She would call merchandisers and managers of stores and tell them who she was and for whom she represented, and the male dominated buyers would drop what they were doing. When she arrived, she did not disappoint. She was seductive without being tactless. She opened and expanded accounts and made money. But she was not in the same place two days in a row. That wore her down. After two years of being in and out of lonely, redundant motel rooms and going home at the end of the week with no one waiting for her while balancing lurid comments and innuendo from the male buyers and associates, Maurine needed a breather.

She had enough money to go to college and finish her art studies. She had a much clearer picture of what she wanted to do. She wanted to structure magazines, and not just girlie magazines. During her time on the road, magazines were her living. She saw what sold and what did not. She decided to use that experience to help make a classy magazine. She plotted a move back to San Francisco. Maurine, however, had a more demanding need, and neither her job nor matriculating in a school could put an ointment on that sore. She had to find her mother.

In 1978, Maurine commenced a concerted effort to track down her mother. There was so little for her to sift through. She had a birth certificate and a less-than-cooperative father who had never added any detail to that portion of her missing heritage. She reluctantly wrote her father and informed him that she was making a point to reach her mother. Mo returned a letter, and surprisingly offered as much information as he had. The details he offered were both dated and incomplete. Mo identified her mother's name as Helena Fuentes Finch. She was from the Bronx, New York. He either could not or he just refused to give insight about Helena's parents or any other family members. She contacted county clerks. She revived talks with her Aunt Rachel, who might have information that would lead her to her mother.

It took her three years of persistence to isolate her mother from thousands of dead-end leads. There was only so much she could have done by herself. She worked a full time job with a magazine and was trying to finish getting her bachelor of fine arts degree at San Francisco State. Two months after finally hiring a private investigator she got confirmation that a woman, Helena Fuentes York, was her mother, in 1981.

Maurine accepted the news of her mother with joy, relief, and guarded anticipation. She prefaced a meeting with a letter, which was answered by Mrs. York. Maurine phoned her from San Francisco, her home since 1978, to Mrs. York's home, just outside of Philadelphia. For as many years as Maurine had longingly dreamed about this conversation, they generated very little to discuss. It was a cumbersome trans-continental telephone reunion, but she hoped that things would improve with a face-to-face meeting. She had located her mother, a brother and two sisters that she had not known existed until that moment. Helena had been married for seventeen years to Henry York, a mailman. Maurine flew east that weekend.

Helena and the family were waiting for Maurine when she landed in Philadelphia. There was no question that Helena and Maurine were related. Maurine was looking at a visage of herself twenty years down the road. Helena was now an attractive 52-year-old with flecks of graying hair. Maurine was slightly taller, but they were built the same. Maurine's skin color was the same as Helena's. Maurine looked far more like Helena than did the other children. Not knowing anything about Helena's past, Maurine could not appreciate the personal accord that her mother presented was cultivated over many years in and out of hospitals and visits with psychologists. Henry, who was the father of only the youngest child, high school senior Neal, was a light-skinned black man in his mid-50s. Neal looked like Henry. Maurine's sisters Kelsey, 22, and Jocelyn, 20, were also light-skinned, and must have taken after their fathers. Maurine spent the weekend at the York home.

The meeting of her newfound family did not prove to be a scintillating experience. Maurine learned some things, like her mother was Puerto Rican and Helena's parents were dead. Helena had a younger married sister who lived in Chicago. But Helena did not feel the urge to divulge much more about herself and her life. Once the initial drama of resurrection played out, a mutual sense of indifference insidiously crept in. It took Maurine's mother most of her adult life and all of Maurine's life, to forget the trauma of her marriage to Mo. Helena was not inclined to relive it with Maurine's presence. Both women were capable of outward displays of affection, but that never materialized here. Her mother had even forgotten Maurine's birth date.

At thirty-two, Maurine was much older than her siblings. They were also raised as part of a family unit. Although they were cordial and curious, they related to Maurine on no particular level. Maurine was saddened by the net effect of her discovery. However, she derived satisfaction that she had a face and a voice to assign her mother. Her mother was barely more a part of her being than was her extinct record collection. She had always identified that as having an inseparable connection to her mom. Maurine returned to San Francisco to continue her life, and pursue her career without the weight of filling in the blanks of her parentage.

Helena and Maurine would move on to respectfully send each other a greeting card on birthdays and Christmas. However, Maurine's psychological being remained conspicuously unfulfilled. Could this have been accentuated by the disappointment conjured during the meeting with Helena? Maurine was streaking toward the pinnacle of her feminine appearance and career ambition. Now her egocentric focus showed that she was not only unmarried but did not have a particular fellow to spark her life.

On her flight back to San Francisco, with the image of her mother fully personified, she toyed in her mind about the "loves" in her life that had come and gone. Overall, this was a temporarily stimulating airborne pastime for her. She spent little time on her experience with Jonas. She directed even less thought to Darrin's father. There were others, the recollections of which were as dim as those relationships were relevant. This cerebral exercise lasted as long as it took for the plane to cross Indiana at 500 something miles-per-hour. She realized neither a successful track record nor an extensive one in the field of romance.

Somewhere in the world there had to be another Chris Mitchell. She sensed that Chris would always be the gauge by which she measured the aching in her heart. Without rushing things, and there was certainly no one to rush to, she felt the internal pressure to get this portion of her life going. She knew that when the plane landed that no one would be waiting for her. There was a limited supply of Chris Mitchells in the world, and in her world, there was none.

Chapter Eighteen *Milestones*

J oe's Tap endured its own changes, but could not keep ahead of the changes of the town. Joe wound his final days down by doing the same thing he had done most of his time at Joe's Tap; he gambled. New Jersey had introduced a statewide lottery, and then later, casino gambling in Atlantic City. This opened the way for Joe and his friends to wager without the threat of arrest. He had been taken to the casinos a couple times, but because of his vision and the congestion in the gaming rooms, he limited his playing to slot machines. He did not have to see the figures in the machines; just rejoice in the results of the ringing bells if he won. When he won, he seldom won big. He never pinned the big jackpot. Joe never found the casinos as interesting as sitting on the side porch with the guys, holding a transistor radio. Listening to horse racing results and giving Maurine a list of his bets to covertly phone in to an illegal bookie proved far more exhilarating. Somehow legalized betting was not as stimulating or as much fun.

At a similar time as the casinos made their mark in New Jersey, Cape May adopted a policy that was as unique as legalized gambling. Cape May was one of the first Jersey shore communities to implement the marketing of beach tags for accessing its beaches. Until the mid-seventies lifeguards, rescue boats, emergency equipment, and any other necessities for beach presentation was a function of the city budget. The tags were sold during the season to anyone going onto the beaches. This salvaged tax money from drowning in the demanding beach operation. Somehow the image of the beach as a personally funded time-share was not met with tremendous support.

This was another consequence of the "urban renewal" movement. The beach was not free anymore and its maintenance was not cheap. Like many of the other changes in town, this one was absorbed by both the locals and the visitors. Eventually beach tags became a part of the vacation time rite of passage. Beach tags became as essential for bathers as barbed hooks and bait were for fishermen. Beach tags reaffirmed Cape May's identity as more upscale in image and practice than Atlantic City or Wildwood. Beach tags were also a euphemism for "more expensive."

Perhaps Joe could have rebuilt Joe's Tap into an off-beach yuppie-drinking haven. In reality, Joe's time and energy had passed him by, and his health was in decline. He entrusted Antonio with the bar tending. However, Antonio was not only undone by another black-oriented bar, catering to a younger crowd just a couple blocks from Joe's Tap, but Antonio was a drug addict. This hampered his business direction. Antonio spent time in drug rehabilitation at a VA hospital while the bar was wheezing its final breaths.

As Joe's health worsened, Mo realized that he was going to lose a wedge, a natural buffer between Mary and himself. He did not want to deal with Mary on an exclusive basis. He was fifty-six and felt he still had a lot of life left; yet he did not want to shine that light on Mary. He gradually eased out of the bar, while finding new watering holes.

Joe who had been in the bar virtually every day for thirty-five years, died in 1980, at age sixty-seven. He was totally blind. Mo finally did leave Joe's Tap, but not because he was despondent over Joe's death. He left because he picked up Mary's sister, Sofia, at Joe's funeral repast. He had already "auditioned" prospective girlfriends, but Sofia looked like what Mary should have or could have looked with a little more commitment like exercise, diet, and make-up. Mary failed to elevate her level of appearance because the men in her life did not challenge her to do so. Joe had been blind and didn't have to see her or touch her. Mo allowed for her unpolished look, while she funded his lifestyle.

Sofia was widowed and the mother of three college age children, which included a set of twins. She was a naturally likeable person.

Mo, who was not adverse to unconventional relationships, said all the right things to Sofia. Sofia was receptive, and Mo gradually moved in with her. Mary's initial ire for both of them proved short-lived.

In a supremely odd twist to Mo moving out, Jerry Strawberry moved in with Mary. He assumed all of the "privileges" formerly afforded to Mo. Mary's relationship with Jerry Strawberry, probably assuaged Mo's fleeing from the bar and her. In practicality, it had been in the works anyway. Mary was twenty-two years older than Jerry Strawberry, and looked it. As Mo drifted away from her, Mary latched onto her rudderless, insecure, drug-addicted employee, Jerry Strawberry--Agent Orange.

Mary died in 1984, a porcine, sixty-one-year-old harridan. Both Joe and Mary could have extended their lives had they been more open-minded about medical care. Joe died of a liver condition. It was the same one that killed Jinx. Joe had given it less attention than Jinx gave his. Mary died from complications attributed to unattended diabetes. Basic modifications in their diets and drinking habits, and a doctor visit or two, could have earned them longer lives.

Antonio spent the considerable parts of 1984 and 1985 getting the demon cocaine monkey off his back. Jimmy Bowersox, had been given clemency for going AWOL, and came back to Cape May from Canada and "ascended" to become the local drug kingpin. Jimmy left his calling card at the bar as he supplied junk for Antonio and Jerry Strawberry, who predictably became reliant on him. The authorities apprehended Jimmy, after a year of intense investigation. Convicted, he was sent off to serve serious time in a federal prison. The judge who sentenced him was a severely wounded Vietnam War hero and did not turn a blind eye (literally) to Jimmy's defection to Canada in considering Jimmy's fate.

When Jimmy went away, Antonio awakened to the immensity of his problem. It was painfully evident that Antonio needed time to heal from his addiction, away from Joe's. He had no one other than Jerry Strawberry to handle Joe's Tap in his stead. It was a "between a rock and a hard place" quandary that did not strengthen the fabric or future of Joe's Tap.

Antonio and Jerry Strawberry would swap stints in drug re-hab and counseling. During Antonio's recoveries, Jerry Strawberry was left to manage the bar. Jerry Strawberry could order the liquor and handle the customers, but he had no concept of bill paying or keeping creditors at bay. Antonio was no better a businessman than was Jerry Strawberry.

After Mary's death, Joe's Tap was Antonio's business. Mary had paid all of the bills from 1945 until she died. She was a tough act to follow, especially if the followers failed to pay the bills and used that money for drugs. Jerry Strawberry's visits to the VA hospital not only helped get him off drugs, but he was also administered for the probable strains of Agent Orange in his system. For the moment, he would survive both afflictions. Medication also helped him shed his upstaging facial tics. As a tandem, Antonio and Jerry Strawberry had a fighting chance to keep Joe's Tap afloat. Individually, the business was doomed to flop. For the better parts of two years in the mid-eighties, as they took turns in re-hab, the business flopped.

The train station that saw so many travelers enter and depart Cape Island, said good-bye to its last train in 1987. Buses and cars following faster, better paved toll ways, rendered locomotive travel to the resort obsolete. Rusting train rails and weather beaten wooden ties that rolled up to the side door of Joe's Tap became the only tangible monument to a century-plus of train travel to Cape May. The city closed Joe's Tap due to back taxes issues in 1986, and razed it in 1989. The façade that anchored the center part of Cape May, the part that never got the front-page kudos, first became a massive pile of bricks, and then an inanimate asphalt lot with parking meters; a lot Mo helped clear. Painted white lines, shaping parking spaces covered the lot where Joe's Tap once reigned.

Early in the 1990s, the city fathers packaged properties, formerly Joe's Tap and the train station, to become part of a Victorian transportation center; a port for horse drawn carriages and tandem bicycles. This lured hordes of vacationers wanting to get a more unhurried view of the city's aesthetics. It also used the enlarged area to be a terminal for tour buses for day-trippers wanting to view the

Victorian homes and get a whiff of the Atlantic. These two missing institutions, neighboring icons of that part of the city, were now banished into lore. Only tales from those who had personally passed through those sites were left to confirm their existence, let alone their former importance and viability.

Joe's Tap was more than a bar. For some, Joe's Tap was home. For some others, it *was* the resort. The train station was more than a depot. It was a yardstick for notching milestones in one's life. Most of the time those milestones were happy. Some people went to the service or college from that station. Many met their loved ones or watched them off from there. Tears of sadness would be waiting for caskets of fallen war heroes who had come home for the last time on the train. The station was gone. Joe's Tap was gone. The final remnants of another time were gone. The centerpiece of a changing community for four decades was gone. The elastic tendrils that held a community together through storms, wars, and social change were gone forever.

During the sixties and seventies, Cape May had relied on tourist business from Canadian travelers. Quebec and Ontario license plates competed with those from New Jersey and Pennsylvania for the paucity of area parking spaces. The money brought into the community was welcomed and liberally spent. The Canadians also offered an expanded cultural footing for Cape May to perform. They were North American, and they respected the American traditions. The sprinkling of the French language gave Cape May an implied continental ambience. Cape May longed to show its European connection, and the French-Canadians contributed to that. However, Canada in the 1980s went through a serious fiscal crisis where its dollar devalued compared to the American dollar and the Maple Leaf pipeline withered on the way to Cape May. The Canadian disappearance heightened Cape May's desire to remain on a multinational cultural stage, but now had no one to impress. By the 1990s Cape Island searched for new markets and visitors that stretched further than Philadelphia or New York.

Overt racism in Cape Island had dissolved, because the attitude of the country had changed. The numbers of black inhabitants had been reduced in the urban renewal make-over. Black people in Cape May voted, and even helped elect an African-American city commissioner. Blacks still did not play a significant part owning Victorian inns, but otherwise worked the same jobs as whites, earning comparable wages. There were just so few blacks to make a difference. None lived in the beach homes. None lived on Montpelier Avenue. Some people drove to Atlantic City to work in the casino industry. In the sixties and seventies, a revealing part of Cape May's association with blacks was the puzzling idea that capable people like Maurine and Chris had to venture to another part of the country to find prosperity. Ironically, by the 1990s, the white kids who had previously caught the crabs and chased the mosquito truck had grown up and were also someplace else. They were not coming back to Cape May either. With Cape May not regenerating its own progeny, the service end of the resort businesses had jobs constantly unfilled. Blacks who in earlier times did this work as a matter of survival; chambermaids in the hotels and motels, as well as kitchen help, vanished. White kids, who never had a shortage of jobs to pick from, worked as much as they desired. The net result was that summer jobs were not fully covered by local talent. New arenas had to be probed for willing workers.

The 1990s saw a new source of summer labor come forth. Cape May, perhaps harking back to its *Mayflower* roots, embraced legions of ambitious British college age kids coming to work in the shops, restaurants, and hotels. These students, primarily women from Ireland, Scotland, Wales, and England found out about Cape May. After the fall of the Soviet Union, Russian kids and other eastern Europeans came to Cape May. They made the flight for a chance to live a summer of moneymaking and fun in America. Somewhere in their enjoying the international nuance of being at an American resort, they would begin to miss their home. This accented the cultural distancing that would eventually surface. In order to combat the inevitable homesickness, many would turn to drinking. They were doing the jobs that the regulars from Joe's Tap did forty years before; work blacks generally had done ever since there was a Cape May. Those jobs had now changed hands, but the drinking remained as the residual distraction.

The idea of having genuine Europeans as working guests in the resort helped fill the void left when the Canadian influence ceased to be a factor. However, these kids ventured through town as hired help, not as paying tourists. The Europeans offered other specialized situations for the community to cope with as well. Their purpose was to work, and much of their work was menial. The big difference from these seasonal migrants and the Joe's Tap regulars was that the regulars had dug their emotional roots into the soil and called it home for as long as they could. Once the adoring locals and vacationers got past the charming British or Russian accents, there was nothing more to bond with among the imported labor force. These kids kept to themselves. They poked fun at the American system while drinking in prodigious portions in their rented houses. Their jaded perspective of American procedure took on a different view from customary summer thought. The British kids soundly brought opinions that were provincially unique and biased.

They could also do childish things that would provoke the established gentry. They would noisily party into the early hours of the morning aggravating local neighbors. On the approaching Fourth of July they could pull small American flags from the front of someone's house and stick the wooden ends into the holes in the hand grips of their loaned bikes like streamers. The ecstasy of having authentic British people doing work in Cape May was reduced with the accompanying youthful irresponsibility. The city was willing to look the other way. Somehow it was more approving to have irreverent, freckled, Irish kids than manageable black folks in town.

Chapter Nineteen *The Will*

M o died in 1991; he was sixty-nine. Maurine lived and worked in San Francisco. Maurine had opted to not remain in close contact with her relations in Cape May. This left her situation as somewhat of a local mystery. In that Mo and Maurine had corresponded during Maurine's search for her mother, Mo had held onto her address. It had not changed during that time. Adele got her address from Sofia, to inform Maurine of her father's passing. She wired the news and money for a round-trip plane ticket. This circumvented any possible money issue for Maurine, not unlike the time she spent with her in Philadelphia, twenty years before.

Initially, Maurine refused to return home for Mo's funeral service. She was saddened by her father's death. However, she was neither overwrought with grief or guilt nor harbored a sense of any unfinished business. Maurine ultimately relented and made preparations to come home. Her reservation about coming was not about money, for she was the corporate marketing director of a West Coast magazine. She had money to travel. Her gut skepticism was about respect. She otherwise resented Mo for not allowing her to have a reasonable childhood or a mother. She fumed every time she thought about her record collection. Once she got home she promptly repaid Adele for the fare.

Ella and Antonio attended Mo's funeral with Maurine. This was the first time since the early 1970s that they all had been together. Previously, Antonio had been to both Joe's and Mary's services. Ella did not come to either one. Today tears flowed, not for Mo, but for the reunion of three kids who grew up as orphans in their parents' home. Mo's funeral snapped the last link to the tormenting rigors of their childhood. Ella came with the McCulloughs and her son Jason. Jason bore a remarkable incarnation of a twenty-five-year-old Joe, but he was larger. He was a non-commissioned officer in the U. S. Coast Guard. Ella had still not found the freedom to admit who Jason's father was. If the subject was broached, she would smartly sidestep it. Ella had not strayed from the McCullough home since her eviction from Joe's Tap.

The McCulloughs deeded Ella a portion of their property. When either Garrett or Sharon would be the last to die, Ella would get the whole farm. Garrett helped her build a small house there with the only stipulation being that she would help the McCulloughs in their old age. That was an easy option for Ella. She remained a line-worker at the laundry, and would never make much money. The love and support that she received from the McCulloughs had been an immeasurable salvation over the years. With the McCulloughs in their early-70s, they had slowed, but were fully capable and needed little assistance from Ella. They just wanted to make sure that she was provided for and nearby.

Antonio had married and was the father of twin girls, two-years-old. He worked construction. After the elimination of Joe's Tap, Antonio began to help Mo with his jobs. Eventually, Antonio got a job with another contractor and worked all the time. He was in conversation with Sofia about Mo's trucks and equipment with an eye on going into business himself. Much of the equipment was almost forty-years-old, but Mo had taken considerable care of his machines. Mo finished servicing them only two weeks before. Antonio was drug-free and wavered on whether he wanted to pursue subcontracting. He saw Mo go stretches without leaving the bar when he preferred to have been running his bulldozer through a muddy lot. Antonio had to stay active for fear of relapsing into a drug-dominated world, from which he had been there and done that.

A poignant sidelight to the ceremony was that Mo's cousin Adele sang at the funeral. Hearing Adele sing not only evoked feelings that Maurine had for Mo, but rekindled the emotions of losing her son, Darrin, twenty years before. She wept for both but it was her remembrance of Darrin, through associating Adele's singing that was the real catalyst.

Adele had recently retired from the factory, and was earning a reasonable pension. She had also inherited her mother's home in West Cape May when Aunt Rachel died in 1988. She had pushed the choir director at her church in Philly for more solo opportunities, and it paid off. Adele's "discovery" at church began a two-decade ride to a level of professional acceptance for her interpretations. Leading up to her retirement, as was her plan, she had gradually become a lounge singer in the clubrooms of Cape May and Wildwood. She had also become a recognized force in the jazz and gospel circuit with recording contracts continually popping up, and a growing legion of fans. This was something that she had dreamed about her entire life. Amazingly, it was the solo at Darrin's funeral where she gained the ultimate confidence to think she could move people with her voice. Her success was an evolving result of her singing for Darrin. She was an emerging star at sixty-five.

Later in the week an attorney read Mo's will. Mo had property holdings, construction equipment, life insurance, and cash. Much of his estate went to Sofia. Mo left Antonio all of his contracting gear. He could use it, sell it, or dump it in the ocean. He even gave money to Jason and Ella. He snubbed Maurine. There was no mention of Maurine, just like she never existed. Maurine was a bit disappointed, but not totally surprised. Mo had borne snubs from Maurine, which she thought were necessary and justified. The fact that she had not been in contact with him since 1977, when she was actively searching for her mother, was the icing on a poorly formed cake, and solidified Mo's disconnect from Maurine. Following the visit with the attorney, Antonio invited Maurine and Ella for a ride around Cape May.

So much had changed over the last couple of decades. The most telling statement they made about that ride was like in Mo's will about Maurine; there was no evidence that Joe's Tap ever existed. This week was the first time Maurine viewed the metered lot where her childhood home used to be. Maurine was happy to ride with

Antonio and Ella. They drove along the beach, and had lunch at a restaurant six stories up overlooking the vast Atlantic. Maurine treated. Cape May had changed so much from what she remembered. They concluded their drive in unanimous incredulity of the condos, motels, and new houses that had sprouted up where poor folks used to live. The classic Victorian houses were spectacularly adorned.

Antonio and Ella dropped Maurine at the motel. She stopped off at the lobby upon her return to check for messages. She had given the phone number to her human resources office if the magazine needed to talk to her. No one else of consequence mattered, since she had just seen Antonio and Ella. There was a note from work for her to call, which she would do as soon as she went to her room. There was a second message from Sofia, her father's girlfriend. Maurine was standing at the front desk trying to figure out why Sofia would call her. She barely knew Sofia. They briefly exchanged condolences at the funeral, but Maurine wanted to find out what Sofia needed.

Chris had taken a circuitous route to get back to Cape May. He never went to law school, he didn't stay married, and he did not keep the job he had with the retail chain. He was working in Philadelphia as an account rep for a wholesale food distributor. This was his third such job since leaving Virginia, in the seventies.

On weekends he would come to Cape May to stay with his aging parents, which got him out of the YMCA room where he lived in during the week. He had no children, but had a girlfriend in Philly that he saw without particular compassion or commitment. The thoughts of idealism and social change that germinated in college had given way to the drudge of day-to-day subsistence. Chris had alimony to deal with and a student loan that had to be paid. Both of these factors hampered his ability to pry himself away from the YMCA and get into law school or pursue an MBA. Chris still had a strong physique, but a spare tire was showing signs of inflating around his belt. His hair was graying, with a gradually widening bald spot; no Afro.

Being careful not to speed on Lafayette Street and get a ticket he could barely pay for, Chris was doing about twenty-five easy miles-per-hour. He had nothing of jarring consequence on his mind except what his mother had cooked for dinner.

With dusk setting the stage for a weekend at the shore, traffic was heavy. The other drivers wanted to get as early a start as they could on their Friday evening festivities. Drivers were equally careful not to antagonize radar guns hiding somewhere along the street. On his right, he saw some of his old buddies with fizzled NBA dreams going four-on-four on the asphalt courts he frequented decades before. In passing, their competition looked like far younger guys who were also larger, faster, and better skilled. He wasn't tempted to play with them, not really.

With only a minute until he got home and with taunting thoughts of his days on the playground, he spotted something in his peripheral vision on his left. Reminiscences of his hoop dreams were rapidly erased. Through the picture window of the Planter Arms Motel, which had Venetian blinds halfway down to block the rapidly setting sun, directly across from the courts, Chris saw the bottom half of a female form at the check-in desk. Chris glimpsed a tight black skirt holding together a pair of shapely black calves. He was almost oblivious to the car in front of him that he was absent-mindedly tailgating. Chris was afforded no other visual information. Something clicked as if those calves were strategically aimed at him. He slowed before he rammed the car. Never to be overly impulsive, and in an uncharacteristic fashion, Chris made an abrupt U-turn in Lafayette Street in his company van; traffic be damned! That maneuver would be just shy of a miracle without traffic. Friday evening had both sides of the narrow street laden with cars. He also flirted with a guaranteed moving violation that would be even more derogatory than a run-of-the-mill speeding ticket, if the police were to stop him. He retreated to the motel and pulled into an empty parking slot. He jumped out of the van and walked purposefully into the lobby. He was not exactly sure what that purpose might be.

The van he drove, the legs he walked on, and his directional sensors were all going in the same direction without cognitive input, except for seeing the legs in the window. He was moving by some impulse, instinct, or intuition of which he had no control, or certainly none that he could relate to. Chris's heart pounded with jackhammer energy through his company-monogrammed pullover shirt. What was he walking into? What was making him do this? He had no answers, yet he could not resist this magnetic force.

The Planter Arms was a small two-story motel that was built in the late 1950s by an African-American, Cape May couple. They sold it last year as they were getting where they had tired of its seven-day grind. This left the bar across the street as the only remaining black owned Cape May business. Chris had never spent time there, for anything. Upon opening the motel door, Chris's eyes locked on a most unlikely illusion. Standing there in the black skirt with the legs that prompted his spontaneous U-turn, was a fully developed and visually captivating Maurine Finch. Their eyes locked for what seemed to be a clumsily long time. This was not exactly like the days at the little store, that used to be just seconds around the corner from the motel, but Chris and Maurine were together again, kind of.

Chapter Twenty *Reunion*

"Maurine, you are not going to believe this…."
"Oh my God…Chris!" She exclaimed. Maurine stepped to Chris and gave a genuine heart-felt hug to someone who had radically moved her in the past. "What's it been, twenty-five years?" Although she had not kept a tally sheet as to the exact lapse in their association, she had a firm handle on how long it had been.

"Yep, I don't think I saw you after I went to college in sixty-six. I know your father died last week, and I was thinking that you might come back, but I didn't know where you were. Maybe that is why I just made that U-turn in Lafayette Street, I have no idea of what I just did!"

"Chris, let me buy you a drink! What are you doing? I'd like to catch up and see what I've been missing for all those years!" Maurine is excited and so is Chris. Maurine is talking faster than Chris can respond. Chris is seeing a carbonated, fizzing, and uninhibited Maurine that he did not get to see while in high school. Chris had never seen Maurine as a full-fledged grown-up. He was as thrilled to see her now as in the days of pretzel rods and puppy love. Looking at her reminded him of why he was so taken by her in the old days. In addition to the tight black skirt, Maurine wore a light blue low-plunging tank top. What a shame that it didn't work out, she is spectacular to watch! "You've got a few minutes to spend with an old friend, don't you?" She insistently asked.

"There's nothing wrong with Sterling's Silver Slipper Lounge across the street. Ever been there?" Chris responded, hoping not to lose track of Maurine this time.

"Let me run to my room for a moment, and make a call. I'll come over. You better be there!"

"No problem!"

Right now, if Maurine told him to wait on the sun, he wouldn't even look for a canteen.

Maurine went to her room to call her work place. She will call Sofia later. Chris left his van in the small parking lot and he crossed the street to the bar. There was a mural on the vast sidewall, splashed in bright footlights, of a black Cinderella-type vixen trying on a silver spike-heeled shoe. He entered the bar. He will wait for Maurine. After twenty-five years, what were a few more minutes? She would not make him wait long.

Maurine and Chris sat at the bar in Sterling's. Four bartenders traversed in the middle of lengthy mahogany bars that ran parallel, with customers facing across from each other. One of the bartenders was none other than Agent Orange himself, Jerry Strawberry. Chris had been in the bar a few times, and knew Jerry Strawberry a bit. Maurine only knew him from when he lived at Aunt Rachel's rooming house in the sixties. Maurine and Chris noticed the youthful faces of the patrons. They realized that they were on the extended upper age range of the median. They knew the parents or big brothers and sisters of the young people who were there. There were six televisions set up around the room. A couple of pool tables were in use, and the jukebox was in continuous reverberating play.

"My gosh Maurine, I saw those legs in the window of the motel and something made me spin around in Lafayette Street. Maybe I recognized them or wanted to recognize them, I don't know what. Something rung a bell. I have never been drawn into anything like that before in my life. It was so weird!" Chris tried to explain. "So where have you been for the last quarter century?"

"First of all, aren't you married?" She asked.

"Well, I guess my question can wait," Chris said with playful sarcasm. "I was for six years, but not now. Maybe I never got over you, huh! I don't see a ring on your finger, either." He lifted her left hand and gazed in mischievous exaggeration.

"Not yet. I live in San Francisco with a pretty cool guy, I suppose. And, you got over me in high school, hello!"

"Oh well, there goes my future again," he said with an un-suppressed chuckle. "Lucky guy!"

"What do you mean? You stopped seeing me in the store a long time ago," Maurine reminded.

"Yeah, but that was not my doing. Mary Di Cicco chased me away from you one day, and made it clear what she meant. And then Antonio returned my silver medal and I figured you wanted me to jump in Island Creek or something. That was my first real broken heart! I was…what should I say, devastated?"

"Say what? I laid my necklace down one day to take a bath, and could not find it when I got out. That damn Mary sent it to you, huh? Ella denied knowing anything about it; I wonder why Antonio did not tell me that!"

Maurine worked on her second Long Island tea, and Chris had his third beer. Between the drinks and in the vibrant atmosphere of the post happy-hour crowd, the jukebox was playing the soulful and romantic Earth, Wind, and Fire *After the Love Has Gone.* Chris excused himself to go to the pay phone to call his mother to put dinner in the microwave oven, as he was going to be late. He did not know how late. As Chris returned to his seat at the bar, he practiced the words that he wanted to say to Maurine. He was too timid to challenge Mary or his father when he was younger, but he knew a long time ago that Maurine was worth the effort. He did not want to fumble this "opportunity."

"I was furious that you did not come to the football dance," Chris told her.

"I don't remember anything about a football dance!"

"Yeah, that was when you sent the medal back. I sent you a letter inviting you to my football dance, when I was a senior. I sent it with Antonio."

Maurine's face fell into a deep frown. "Excuse me," she said, "I have to make a phone call. I have to call Antonio, and I've been with him most of the week. I'll buy you another drink, don't go anywhere!" Maurine is trying to piece the parts of her life together that are both fuzzy and disturbing. Chris waited with a fresh beer. He chatted with folks that passed. Maurine was gone for 10 minutes and returned.

After twenty-five years of varying degrees of success and happiness, Maurine came back with a disheartened look. "He remembered. He said he was supposed to deliver a letter to me, from you. Mary saw him coming to my room and asked him what he was doing. She took the letter from him, and told him to do something. She must have come into my room then and took the necklace, I guess. That night she told him to give you a package and not to tell me about it. He didn't know what was in the package. She also told him to say that I couldn't go to the dance. Jesus, I never knew about any of this!" She detailed.

"Do you know why I stopped coming by the store?" Chris asked.

"I bet Mary had something to do with it, huh?"

"She stopped me in the street one day and told me to stay away from you. What's more, I think she called my dad or something. He told me to quit seeing you too!" By this time, Chris is drinking Jack Daniel with ginger ale and Maurine is on her fourth Long Island tea.

They both were gigglers when they got drunk, and were having fun reliving a strange part of their lives that harshly affected them, then and now. They giggled like little kids watching Tom and Jerry cartoons.

"Antonio also told me that his Aunt Sofia left a message for me. I'll call her tomorrow. She was Mary's sister. I meant to call her earlier, but I lost my focus. The less time I take to think about unnecessary matters the more clearly I can think about stuff when it does matter. You are what I want to think about. You have always mattered."

"Thanks for saying that. I never really understood what your situation was at Joe's Tap. I just knew that I liked you and was scared of Mary and that Cujo-looking collie."

"Oh Chris, you just don't know how much I liked you! Do you remember the walk on the beach?"

"Yeah, the absolute highlight of my life!"

"Oh stop, you always said things that I liked. But you said that we were perfect. I distinctly recall saying wait until we are forty and make that judgment. My God, we are past forty!"

"So what do you think?" He asked.

"Maybe we are. You still have the body, and still have the wit, you know! What about me?" Maurine replied.

"You are different. You are grown up. You are bigger in places that are really awesome." Chris is staring squarely at Maurine's ample cleavage. "You are smarter than hell. And you are more confident. Do you realize that I have never been out with you around people? We had to sneak around just to go to the beach! And darn, you don't stop talking now. I think back in the day, you were either scared of me or afraid to let your hair down, if you will. You talked, but not with the enthusiasm that you do now."

"Life is full of what-ifs!" Maurine lamented. Maybe I was afraid of a lot of things. Life's experience helps one become more capable of dealing with some of those issues. I was afraid of losing you, huh. And it happened anyway."

Maurine and Chris sat and talked. They recalled the parts of their lives that they shared, and the quarter of a century with no contact with each other. They both agreed that it should not have happened that way. Maurine mused, "How can someone have so much fun after burying her father, and getting snubbed in the will? I don't know, but I am!"

They meshed. They had always meshed. This was too cool to let pass without posing out loud about "what happens next?" They both feared the answer. Maurine left on Sunday, back to her life and back to her boyfriend. Chris would head back to Philly on Sunday, to the YMCA.

Midnight came quickly, and the minutes were already liberally trickling through Saturday's hourglass; methodically stealing precious moments from this long awaited but unanticipated reunion. This could be the shortest day of their lives. Chris walked Maurine back to the motel. They kissed at the door to her room. This was not a peck-on-the-cheek good night kiss, but a real tongue swapper.

Chris told her that he would like to come by in the morning and take her to breakfast, "and see what you look like in the daylight!"

They felt the same way they did on the beach in the summer of '64, like this had to stop; that they were not fully exempt from the black cloud that stalked them before. However, the essence of their connection seemed like it will never change. In twenty-five years, they both had changed, but in so many ways they had not climbed off each other's wavelength. Chris tendered her good night and got into his company van to go find his dinner in his mother's microwave. He drove by the iconic little store which was now vacant on his drive home.

Maurine, who was still programmed on Pacific Time, took a shower. She knew what drunk was, and she was just that. In the privacy of the motel shower, she was giddy and giggling and like so many times in her life, alone. She is not tired or sleepy, but was searching for solutions to what could be a legitimate perplexity in Saturday's daylight. Maurine's reluctant visit home was now complicated by an irresistible urge to find out more about Chris. There was nothing left of her youth, there was no family with whom she could readily align her past. Antonio and Ella were something like family; they were brother and sister, but not hers. What was she to them? Her mother had buried her forty years ago. Her late father had buried her fourteen years ago. San Francisco was where she lived, and even called home. But it was not her dream home. Not yet.

Chris did not have a car or an apartment of his own. But he made her laugh and elevated her soul. Improbably, and after twenty-five years and four exhilarating hours, they had rediscovered each other. He always wanted to be with her; she did not want to lose him again. A major roadblock for both of them was the boyfriend waiting for her to come home, on the other side of the country. She stretched out on her bed and gave thought to a reawakening of something special. Could it be that special? That was a question she had always asked. Chris would return at ten o'clock and she would be ready, she would find out.

While her heart was beating for Chris, her mind flew back to California. Maurine had an off and on relationship in San Francisco with a guy that was as much off as on. She had been living with him for the last five years. Neither of them felt the urgency to marry. She had given thought to removing him on more than one occasion. Her reluctance for not pursuing matrimony revolved around his battles as a manic-depressive, peppered with his inconsistent declaration to overcome it.

Her roommate, but not soul mate, was a fifty-five-year-old high school administrator. Wil Park was a vice principal, and had been in charge of discipline at the same school for the last decade. Wil expressed his frustration for not ascending to a principal's position in the school district. He also had a penchant for bringing his stressful work home with him. His behavior had shaken the foundation of their relationship like a seven point spike on the Richter scale in the San Andreas Fault. They actually lived through the earthquake of 1989 without enduring any severe property damage. Ironically, Maurine's first San Francisco residence in Western Addition underwent serious structural damage and was immediately razed.

Wil had been married twice, but was now widowed. His children were grown, and were about as close to him as Maurine had been to her father. Wil had many positive accomplishments in his life in teaching, coaching, and church. However, his excitable temper had driven his kids away. This was solidified when his first marriage ended in divorce. He came thoroughly undone with the death of his second wife in a traffic accident. He had been married for less than a year. Mired in an emotionally trying imprisonment, Wil's temperament needed repair. Following the death of his second wife, Wil found another relationship for about two years. Viola Seale was a young widow and a devout church-goer. She even had a reasonably civil relationship with Wil's children. This was something that wasn't apparent during his second marriage. Wil was impressed by her looks and piety as she often quoted the Bible and opted not to indulge in anything more than some light petting with Wil. Wil was about to ask her to marry him when she announced that she was engaged to the minister of the church. Wil was blindsided to the nth degree.

How could he not see that? With Wil pressing the issue, he found out that the minister had been regularly picking the lock to Sister Viola's "chastity belt" while he was relegated to holding her hand and being told to "wait."

For Wil and Maurine money was a non-factor in their relationship, as they did very little with it. They both had great incomes and a substantial amount of identity in their careers. Maurine had been with the successful magazine, and imparted a heady part of its image since she hired on as an art and photography contributor in 1978. Her drive and insight helped create the magazine's personality, even though she did not begin as a high level employee. Maurine earned a bachelor's degree in design and marketing from San Francisco State in 1982, while working full time. During that time is when she became fully immersed in the search for her mother.

She rapidly elevated through the ranks to become the Corporate Marketing Director. She owned an undersized condo in Western Addition, and drove a 1984 Mercedes-Benz, that she bought new. Her vacations were a couple days driving the Coast Highway to visit friends and watch the Pacific waves with seals cavorting. She went to Puerto Vallarta, Mexico, with some girlfriends but that was seven years ago. She liked being in San Francisco, and had maintained many of the same eclectic friends for almost twenty years.

Maurine knew Wil Park's second wife from church; they were about the same age. Maurine also was in church groups with Sister Viola and Wil. Maurine knew the devastation of losing someone in a dramatic and unexpected way. The impending marriage of his "girlfriend" to the preacher presented as complete a test of sanity as one man should endure, especially one with a shaky foundation. Wil and Maurine rapidly gravitated to each other through their opposite natures. Maurine had a soft spot for puppies, kittens, and the brokenhearted, and Wil was a drenched, shivering, stray looking for a plate of milk and needing his head patted. As she had done in the past for people with problems, Maurine consoled Wil, and their relationship grew.

Maurine found Wil's behavior rude and intimidating, at times, while justifying it as part of his grief and frustration. After recurring periods of nice-nice, Wil would go into inexplicable periods of foul-humor and verbal abuse. When Maurine would move to get him out of the house, he would clean up his attitude, and become the poster child for fondant sweetness.

Complicating the emotional frustrations for Wil was that his blood pressure was high. He had recently become diagnosed with diabetes and was taking insulin shots. He was also in sporadic pain from an arthritic condition. The resulting physical and emotional composition of Wil had subjected him to sustained periods of sexual impotence. Maurine recognized that Wil had problems, and initially sought to help him through them. Wil's unevenness contributed to hers. When Wil showed his evil side, Maurine would predictably refer to her liquor cabinet.

Maurine had always carried an awareness of the ills of alcohol. She also felt that she could be overcome by it, if she let it. She was fully conscious of her desire to drink when Wil went into his moody, Mr. Hyde imitation. Wil lived there, but he did not have a lifetime lease on the condo, or on Maurine's heart. Wil had a house in the East Bay area that one of his kids and her family lived in. By now, Maurine did not need another outburst to ask him to get out; she certainly did not expect him to handle it well, when she did. Maurine had never deftly handled loneliness, in spite of the happy-face that she put on, and solitary confinement is what would inevitably result if she preemptively jettisoned Wil. As solid as her professional life had proved, her personal side was far less stable. Life was only as strong as the options one creates, and she had not fully allowed herself the luxury of nurturing such options; until reuniting with Chris.

Chapter Twenty-One
OK, What Now?

Saturday was the first day of autumn. Tomorrow would be the day that Maurine goes back to San Francisco. On this particular Saturday morning the temperature will be in the high 70s with a bright cloudless sky. This is the kind of day the Victorian promoters had been selling to the world since the mid-sixties. The weather can't get any better than this!

Chris arrived at the motel at 10 a.m. and knocked on the door. He was casually attired with a blue pullover shirt and blue shorts. He wore blue and gray running shoes with no socks. He had on a blue baseball cap. At least by now, he was more concerned with his dressing than he was when he was younger. Maurine opened the door to the first floor room.

"Hey stranger! Let me grab my purse and we'll go." Maurine picked up her handbag and closed the door. She took little notice of the fact that Chris dressed better these days. But Chris's mode of transportation was not exactly a hi-tech chariot. They both headed for Chris's paneled company van. It had the logo of a food company on its doors. They drove to a hotel on the beach that offered a weekend breakfast buffet until eleven. Even as the season wound down, the sun-filled Saturday was going to have the beaches busy with late-season bathers.

They got their fill of food and sat at a table with a red and white checkered tablecloth. It was quiet in the room with just a few couples eating. Chris loaded his plate with eggs, hot cakes, bacon, and sausages. Maurine seemed satisfied with a small tomato juice and an English muffin. "You don't eat very much," observed Chris. "I try to eat more than it costs for these places to have a buffet. I want to get more than my money's worth!"

"I'll get more in a moment, but I am a little queasy from drinking last night," Maurine admitted.

"I just want you to feel OK," said Chris.

"Well good, thanks. By the way, it was fun riding in the van," Maurine quipped.

"It's temporary. I am currently in between repossessions!" he joked. "The van doesn't cost me anything and I get a new one in another three months."

"Repossessions?" She muttered.

"Yeah, I got into a...how do you say it...cash flow problem, and had to get a job with a car, if you will!" Chris told her.

"So is this what you want to do, drive around in a company van? Or do you aspire to have your own car some day?" Maurine probed, as she sipped the tomato juice that was the perfect nectar for the hangover she sported. Maurine always had a knack of counseling folks with sensitive issues.

"Actually, I have to find a place that I want to live, and perhaps someone I want to live with, and then I'll worry about a car. But yeah, I want to get a car and the note that goes with it," he conceded. "I usually don't have glamorous riders in the van. At least you did not complain about me just having AM radio."

"So where do you want to live? Cape May? Philadelphia?" Maurine continued.

"I figured it out, just now! I've never been to the West Coast; I'll live in San Francisco with you and your boyfriend. How's that?" Chris said that in jest, but he was looking for a reaction from Maurine.

"So when are you coming?" Replied Maurine, she also sought a reaction.

"I'll tell you what, if the boyfriend wasn't part of the equation, I'd be there! They got jobs out there?"

"You're educated and you have a sizeable personality. You have been in sales a bunch of years. You could get a job easy. Not only that, I know where those jobs are. You'd make more money than you are making now. I would make sure of that! Life is what you ask for, and you should ask for more. You deserve more than living at the YMCA and driving around in a company van."

"So what about the boyfriend?" Chris asked.

"Chris, let me say it this way, if your new car is parked in my driveway, there is no room for his!"

"Hmm!" Is all Chris could mutter. This choked off all sense of eating his breakfast. He sat across from Maurine, and cannot believe she said that.

"Let's just enjoy this day, and see how we feel once we get away from each other. Who knows, I might not see you for another twenty-five years!" Maurine pondered.

"If that is the case, then at least that is something between you and me, not anybody else deciding that. I trust what we can do. However, if it is another 25 years, you'll still only be 67!"

Maurine was heartily laughing at Chris's speculative mathematics, but she had basically placed an offer squarely on the table for Chris to think about--and for her to think about as well. "I called Sofia this morning, and she said that she has something for me. Would you mind taking me by her place? She lives out by the lighthouse," Maurine requested. "I spoke to her at the funeral, but I don't really know her. I don't think she lived around here when I was growing up."

"Of course, whenever you are ready to leave, but I want to show you this first," said Chris. He pulled out his wallet as if to retrieve his credit card to pay for the meal. "Remember this?" He asked.

From his wallet Chris removed Maurine's high school graduation picture and showed it to her. A photo of dubious outcome, the one she had mailed him. It had been living in Chris's wallet for almost a quarter century.

Maurine is totally astonished that Chris actually got the picture, let alone kept it on him. "No way!" Was all Maurine could say.

"I guess I always wanted to contact you and let you know what I was doing, but Mary scared me, then I got a girlfriend, who I married. But even when I was married, that picture stayed in my wallet. I don't get wallets all the time, but that picture was the first thing I transferred when I did. Maybe I'd still be married if it hadn't meant so much to me. She told me to get rid of it, and I didn't; she split."

Chris's sincerity and devotion was made alarmingly clear to Maurine. She was stunned. "No way," she voiced a couple times. "No way could you have done that!"

"I mean, there were other reasons that the marriage did not work, but until right now, I never thought how much you meant to me, even then. I just thought I was being, you know, sentimental. Damn!"

They finished their breakfast with more complications to their lives than when the day started, but they both were happy to have had this conversation. There were many things that remained to be uncovered about the other; nobody sits still for twenty-five years. However, the only unanimous truth either of them considered was that they both cared for the other; immoderately cared.

Chris chauffeured Maurine to Sofia's home in Cape May Point. Her house was a semi-mansion, built in the 1970s. The waves of the ocean crashed on the beach only about a hundred yards behind her house, just beyond a man-made dune. Her home and the beach were connected by a wooden walk. She had a big collie racing in her yard that is the spitting image of Benito. The dog was playfully barking, announcing the visitors. There were trees and flowers landscaped around the large yard. Seagulls lofted over the house. The lighthouse was the neighborhood skyscraper and was just down the block. This area had few existing Victorian houses, as most of the houses were more *nouveau*. Many of the older homes had been clobbered by the encroaching waves and the weather, over time. Because of that much of the community had to be rebuilt. Barrier dunes were created to protect the new homes.

Sofia was in the yard and greeted Maurine and Chris. Seeing the imitation Benito and noting Sofia's considerable facial resemblance to Mary and Carmen, gave Maurine a *déjà vu* kind of feeling, but this was no taproom. She called the dog, "Benedict." Maurine sensed her father's influence in naming the dog.

Sofia gave Maurine a hug. Maurine introduced Chris to Sofia. Sofia took them into the house. She had varnished hard wood floors that reflected the glistening midday sun penetrating through a large window. She had pictures of her children and grandchildren throughout. On the light-green papered wall was a picture of Sofia and Mo. Maurine had not seen her father in a long time, except in the coffin, and realized that he had aged pretty reasonably on Sofia's watch. The wood-framed picture also punctuated an obvious happiness that blessed Mo in his final days, and the apparent joy that he brought to Sofia. After a tour of the house, Sofia took them up a winding set of steps to a crow's nest protruding through the attic, with a marvelous view of the ocean. She offered them a pair of binoculars to scan the horizon.

Sofia was in her late 50s, maybe 60. She was nothing like Mary; she was more like the people Maurine had become accustomed to in Western Addition. Sofia was a positive, svelte, and attractive woman. Her husband died seventeen years ago from a rampaging bout with prostate cancer. He was beset with it for about seven years leading up to his death. Sofia had spent the bulk of her adult life being a housewife in Florida. She sold her husband's share of a construction business, and coupled with the proceeds from the life insurance moved three miles from her childhood home.

Sofia was currently hurting from the loss of her mate, Maurine's father, and had too many rooms in the house not to be constantly reminded of her solitude. She was still in serious mourning. Sofia was miserable not having anyone around. However, she did not let her grief dominate her character.

She wheeled a cart of snacks and beverages onto the deck which also offered a wonderful view of the ocean, and the three of them sat under an umbrella. Their snacks were eaten off a custom crafted wrought iron table as they sat on matching chairs that surrounded the table. Then Sofia got down to business.

"I am happy that you could come to Mo's service," she told Maurine. "I know that you and Mo had problems, but I don't want you to think that he did not care about you. He did care. He lived here for ten years. I don't know how he put up with my sister for all those years, but that was their thing." Sofia's physical mannerisms and command for a situation were similar to Mary's. Her sexiness was more refined than the bawdier Carmen. Her engaging presentation was far more compelling and endearing than both of them combined.

Chris revived the appetite he lost earlier. He ate the sandwiches and potato chips, and drank a chilled ginger ale. Maurine's attention was squarely on Chris and less on Sofia. Maurine also wondered how Chris kept a decent physique with all of the food he attacked, and asked, "Chris, just how do you maintain your figure with all of the food you consume?"

Her question was prompted because Chris had almost single-handedly destroyed a breakfast buffet only about an hour before.

"Well, living at the Y has its advantages. I lift weights and play basketball just about every day. Actually, I've lost about 45 pounds in the last year. I am glad that you did not get to see me for the last half dozen years. I was a freaking hippo."

Maurine embraced that Mo was fortunate to have Sofia late in his life. Sofia waited for Chris to sum up his workout regimen and continued explaining Mo's posthumous message, "Mo wanted me to give you this, but only if you came to his service; and I thank you for coming." Sofia handed Maurine a large manila envelope with Maurine's name on the front in Mo's printing. Maurine opened the envelope. Mo had a handwritten script letter addressed to her, and a document, inside. She looked at the document. It was a life insurance policy for $50,000, with Maurine as the beneficiary. Maurine was floored. Her attention had now been thoroughly redirected to Sofia.

After growing up in Cape Island with memories that were best kept shielded from her consciousness, Maurine was overwhelmed with surprises, which took a while to find her. The potent contributions by Chris and her father were beyond comprehension. She proceeded to read the letter, which said:

Aug. 2, 1989
Dear Maurine,
I hope you are doing well. As you can tell, I've had better days. I am leaving you the insurance that's in this envelope. The only one I cared about coming to my funeral was you. I told Sofia that if you came, I'd give you some things. Taped in the envelope is a key. Go to the garage and open that crate with the lock. The only thing I was disappointed about was you did not let me meet my grandson. But I am sure there are things that I upset you with. Have a good life.

Good-bye,
Daddy (J. Maurice Finch)

Maurine was in tears, and Sofia began to weep just watching Maurine. Chris massaged Maurine's neck and shoulders. After a couple of silent tear-filled minutes Maurine said, "I have to look at something in the garage, a crate of something." Chris took a final sip of ginger ale and Sofia led them down the steps to the garage.

There was a padlocked unadorned wooden crate toward the rear of the two-car garage that housed Sofia's Jeep Grand Cherokee and Mo's late model GMC pick-up. Maurine had no idea what could be waiting for her, but the suspense was intense. She felt the same way when Chris gave her the medal, oh so many years ago. It was a sizeable crate.

Maurine unlatched the lock with the key. She lifted the hinged top open. Embedded in a bevy of wadded newspaper were, of all things, her old phonograph records, the 45s. She pushed the paper around to see how many of the records were there. It looked like the entire lot. They were in their respective albums, along with her log and notes cataloguing each record.

"Oh my God!" she exclaimed.

"Mo told me that he never sold the records. Mary tried to sell them a couple of times, but he wouldn't let her. Mo told me the last time he had the collection appraised, they were worth between ten and twelve thousand dollars. He was aware of their value a long time ago. The value has gone up because as I understand they are not making records like this anymore, and the collection is so enormous. That was in 1987 when he moved them here," Sofia explained. "I have the card of the collector, right here." Sofia handed Maurine the business card.

Maurine had always used the records as a source to relate to her mother. It is more likely they helped find her father. Why did he do this? Maurine was totally consumed with emotion. Those records had meant so much to her, and understood Mo to say that they were long gone. What could she do with them now?

"Sofia, I did not expect this," said Maurine, after stealing a moment to regain her composure. "I have no place to store them, and I had never given thought to selling them. These records were never about money. Could I park them here until I figure out what I can do?"

"Maurine, you are Mo's daughter. You grew up with my niece and nephew. You are family in every sense of the word. Please, leave them here as long as you care to. I doubt that I will ever move, unless the ocean has other ideas. I will even put it in my will that if they are here when I die, that they belong to you and no one else! The only thing I suggest is that you get them insured."

For Maurine things spun around in a dizzying way. She could never have prepared for all that was happening, and there was no one to consult for help. With Mo gone and her mother revealed, there was so little sentiment left in the rediscovery of the records. In some ways there was a sense of guilt seeping in that she did not have more of an ardent resolve to do more with the collection. The only one she could now assign an emotional association with those records was Mr. Elmo. Maybe she could give him a call and see how he was doing.

"I am so much out of time to do anything. I will contact this collector to try to get a market value, either for sale or insurance, and I will write you as soon as know what I am doing. This is such a total shock!" Maurine exclaimed.

"Certainly, dear! And while I have your attention, I am hoping that you and Chris would like to come to dinner here this evening. I used to barbecue with Mo all the time, now he is not here. I would enjoy having your company. How does ribs and chicken sound? Maybe it is not too late to get Antonio and Ella over." Sofia gushed with anticipation.

Maurine glanced at Chris, and he gave an emphatic nod, yes. "Sure, we'd love to, what time?" Maurine checked.

Both Chris and Maurine wanted to retrace their maiden voyage in the sand of the beach, and they had not even presented that idea to the other. Chris inquired, "Can I leave the van right here, and Maurine and I go for a walk? You get pretty good weather out here on Cape May Point, and I think a walk will do us some good right now!"

Maurine was keen in her agreement with Chris, and said, "That is just what I was going to say. We'll walk the beach for a couple hours." Beach tags are neither necessary after Labor Day, nor were lifeguards employed after the holiday, even as many bathers cavorted in the surf.

"Let's say dinner is served between five-thirty and six. You go and enjoy the beach. If you come back early, we can sit and talk some more. I have four bathrooms. I have plenty to eat, and there is so much I want to find out about what you both do. So go have fun!"

Sofia's gracious disposition was a far cry from Mary's Machiavellian demeanor, even in her time of sadness.

Chris and Maurine bade Sofia good afternoon, and they headed back in the opposite direction from their epic walk in 1964. This walk was from the lighthouse to the cove. Maurine had a straw sun hat, sunglasses, and a matching canary yellow blouse and shorts. She had a pair of casual Birkenstock shoes that work much like expensive flip-flops because they had no heel straps. The shoes came off and they darted into the water where the rolling waves came to rest. They were so much more at ease with themselves than earlier in their lives. Maurine was euphoric, and Chris was a major part of it. There are other people on the beach, of whom they barely took notice.

Chapter Twenty-two *The Nap*

Chris and Maurine romantically rummaged the beach looking for "their" sand dune. It was not their intention to go and make-out, like teen-agers, but a dress rehearsal to the re-start to their "what-if" relationship. They both recalled the feelings of young love, but could not remember just where the dune was. In twenty-seven years, the ocean can have a disruptive authority on an adjacent landscape, just like how time erodes memory. Not only was that sand dune gone, but also that entire section of the cove had been carved away. Neither of them realized that. Things looked different, but all sand dunes had a similar DNA helix!

They found a sand dune and adopted it as their personal monument, without authenticating its genesis. It was a surrogate keystone to something that proved to be important in the past, and resumed in its importance for them, today. They romped along the water in the hot sun following a night of drinking. Maurine had eaten very little and was beginning to feel ill. The emotional immensity of the events of the week and a sun-stained hangover were culminating in a big-time tummy ache.

Chris suggested that they go back to Sofia's so Maurine could lie down until dinner. Maurine agreed. They walked back in soothing ankle deep ocean water. Maurine periodically reached down to pick up a handful of the salty water to splash upon her face. Their retreat was slower and with more direction than their splashing to the ill-fated dune. Although it was a beach Saturday, the nuns at the convent next to the lighthouse were mobilized and going for walks in the neighborhood. They dressed in their summer white habits and marched in double-file headed for an apparent afternoon in the sun. The lighthouse may be the commanding structure of the area, but the convent housed its moral conscience. Chris looked at the sisters leaving the retreat. While keeping a close watch on Maurine's condition Chris wondered out loud, "Where do the nuns go for kicks? They just can't frolic on the beach in those outfits!"

Maurine was more profound.

"I know I shouldn't drink," Maurine said.

"Why, are you an alcoholic or something?"

"I hope not, but who knows? I have been around drunks and alcoholics most of my life. I just know that drinking causes more problems than it cures. But I don't act any smarter than those people I used to see in the bar."

Maurine clutched Chris's hand and began to feel better as they neared Sofia's. The lighthouse peered out to sea, right over their heads, staunchly standing guard above the shore. It was easily the tallest and most venerable structure in the area. They climbed the wooden walk toward the house, and approached the fenced yard. Benedict raced at them, but did not possess the sullen, ferocious, personality that Benito did if aliens came into his yard.

Sofia barbecued on the deck while sipping a Diet Pepsi and welcomed Maurine and Chris back. Chris told Sofia that Maurine was ill and needed to lie down. Sofia promptly escorted them to a spare bedroom with an adjoining bathroom. Although Sofia was a trained registered nurse, there was nothing about Maurine's condition that alarmed her. She offered Maurine a couple aspirin and dutifully returned to her grilling. Her company freshened up and went into the bedroom for a nap. It was three-fifteen, and two plus hours before dinner.

Sunlight and salt air layered on an alcohol bender will zap energy. Maurine laid down on the quilted comforter atop the queen-sized bed. They did not turn on the air conditioning, but a breeze drifted in through the screened windows. Maurine was spent. Chris was also tired, and took his shirt off and reposed on the bed as well. They drifted off to sleep--in the same room, on the same bed. For all of the lonely times they had privately thought about the other, the closeness of their bodies failed to register. In moments, they both are doing some hard-core snoring.

Maurine closed the distance between her and Chris. She nestled next to him in an instinctive feminine reaction to being with someone she adored. Chris was still snoring. He thought that he was in a dream. In between loud bursts of nasal grunts and growls, he dreamed of Maurine. This was not the first time that he had dreamt about Maurine, but never was it with her on the same bed with him breathing on his neck. It took him a bit to wake up to the fact that Maurine was right there, but he did. Chris awakened to the realization that he was with the one she wanted. She was the one he had *always* desired. In the bedroom of Sofia's house, he continued from where he left off behind the sand dune in 1964. This time she neither smacked his hand nor demanded a report card.

They fondled, explored, and generally satisfied every sensual curiosity that they had about the other with an almost corybantic intensity. Maurine's canary outfit was off. Everything was off. The nakedness of Maurine's body exemplified what a woman of any age would love to look like. Chris took all of this in and responded to her unlike he had to any woman he had ever met.

Maurine was planning, in her mind, Chris's new car in her driveway. Chris, by now, hoped not to be around when issued his next company van. He had never been to the West Coast, and it was never even on his things-to-do list. His list had just taken on a whole different priority order, and it seemed that Maurine was on every page of it. Their moments of blissful romance were jolted a bit when an excited Benedict began barking.

Antonio had arrived. Squeezed into his extended cab pick-up truck were his wife Allison along with Jason, Ella, a 71-year-old Carmen, and his identical twin daughters, Maura and Maureen. With the conversation from the deck soon entering the room, Chris and Maurine prepared to join them. Maurine pondered her flight, which left in exactly one day. Could the next twenty-four hours possibly compare with the last twenty-four? It was not likely that any twenty-four hour period could be equal to the one she just experienced, but if Chris was in the picture she could be more positive in thinking that something great could happen.

For Chris, he could not be sure how Maurine could be so forward about his coming to San Francisco. Her offer opened passageways that Chris had not traveled. If she proved to be serious, he would go there. He had short-circuited on a number of things in his life, but dealing with Maurine was not something that he botched up on his own. If such a life is what he asked for, like she told him existed, then he was asking for Maurine. If he got a second chance, he would grab it.

Chapter Twenty-three
What If?

The clock ticked away the final moments of the festive barbecue at Sofia's. Maurine had recounted a quarter of a century that contained many previous untold moments, fortified from those with whom she had grown up. Each member of the group had survived difficult affronts to their personal lives, and found redemption, of sorts, in handling their respective challenges. The clock was also ticking on Maurine. Maurine had watched the interplay of Allison and Antonio, with their two young girls.

The girls played with Maurine until they all got exhausted. They were so energetic. Allison, who Maurine did not know, leaned over to her and said, "You know Antonio named them for you, don't you?"

"That's right Little Mo," said Antonio. "You never judged me about anything, and I was screwed up for a long time. I knew you were going to be something, and I want my girls to have your strength of character. I know what you went through!"

Ella, who had overcome as much as anyone there, sat quietly by beaming at being with Maurine, her son, mother, aunt, brother, and nieces. This was the most complete formation of a family as she had ever known.

At forty-two, Maurine knew that her time was running out on having the kind of life that she had thought so much about when she was younger. The kind she witnessed from Antonio and Allison. She had not shared the information with any of them, that she had been a mother for seven months in the 1971. Noting Antonio's kids and seeing how proud Ella was of Jason revived those disquieting, lingering, and maternal cravings. This was a part of her life over which she had no control. She saw the diminishing of opportunity available to her. It was the ticking of a biological clock that would soon run out of its natural fuel, and ferment in the bowels of the "what-if" world. She had clarified for herself some things that may have hindered her progress in her own personal direction. Specifically, there was no past, and there was no clear-cut future; there was only now. Wil Park was not part of her "now." She determined Chris Mitchell was her "now." She had to make sure that he understood that. She wanted a child and she wanted Chris to be a major reason for it.

The clock was surely ticking on Chris and Maurine spending any more time together, for this weekend. It was eight-thirty and the sun had gone down over the ocean, forty-five minutes ago. Carmen and Sofia chatted away like sisters who didn't get around each other very much and were trying to catch up on the past, and paid little attention to the night air. The temperature had dropped with the disappearance of the sun. Antonio's daughters were getting sleepy and cranky. Despite Sofia's exuberant hosting, it was about that time to say good night.

Chris and Maurine had spent the day together from ten in the morning, yet they did not want to let go. After making sure that everyone had proper phone numbers and addresses, Chris and Maurine departed the gathering in the company van that had sat in front of Sofia's all day. Chris offered to drop Maurine off at the motel while he went home to change his clothes, and say hello to his folks. Maurine would change too, and they would meet at ten-fifteen at her room. They would then decide their encore events of the night. As much as they had found out about the other, they both wanted to know more.

Chris returned at quarter past ten, and they chose to walk on the Promenade. They disdained the lure of the bars and nightclubs. By now, drinking was both pointless and played-out. The evening was cool--romantically cool. It was the kind of night that required a warm body to huddle next to while walking, as the moonlight coursed through the fresh autumn wind. Chris and Maurine slowly strode the Promenade with a sense of realized destiny, aside the beating heart they had craved since high school. They acted like tourists and stopped in a couple Promenade shops for hooded sweat shirts and then for some mixed nuts.

Maurine and Chris sat on the Promenade bench; it was about 200 yards from the one that Chris was waiting for Maurine on that fateful day a long time ago. The briskness of the air was simply a functional excuse they both used to hold on that much tighter. Peering into the darkness of the Atlantic, they watched the sky light up with volatile bolts of electricity, silhouetting far away clouds into natural sculptures of art. That remote lightning did not impact on Chris and Maurine; it provided the nautical backdrop on an otherwise star freckled night. "Well Chris, I came home to bury my father, and wound up falling in love--with you!"

"Yeah, and I came home to get some spaghetti, reheated in the microwave, and I see your legs in the window of the motel. I still marvel at that. That still...How is that for great luck, huh?"

"I have had a very lucky week. There was a time I could not wait to get away from here, and there was never really a time that I felt like I needed to come back. I am sorry, but I did not break the doors down at the travel agency when my father died. But in this last week, I have seen so many things about Cape May and about myself, that I never gave thought to before," Maurine allowed in between munches on cashews and almonds.

"Like why so many people really care about you?" Chris asked. "I have always cared for you. I just wish that I had the guts to let you know that, before we got so side-tracked with our lives, and all!"

"Well the people who manipulated my life are not here any longer. Chris I am forty-two. I have done a lot of things, and been to different places, but today is possibly the most meaningful day of my life."

"Whoa, that's deep!" Chris said.

"I found that my father loved me, in his own odd kind of way. I got my record collection back. I had given up on those twenty years ago. You can't imagine how much I hurt because I thought that was gone. I still can't believe that I have it back. I hung out with Antonio's kids and Ella's son. Antonio and Ella do things with their kids, and I am so happy that they can. I know where they came from, and I am so proud of them to be able to have a loving relationship with their children. And of course, there is you. Maybe I have a new focus on what I want from my life!" Maurine's thoughts are at times competing with the pounding waves that are becoming more aroused. She had to raise her voice a bit to overcome the sound of the surf, even as she rested her head on Chris's shoulder. He absorbed every word.

The lightning that was so far away a moment ago was easily looming closer, and merited more than a passing notice from Maurine. People with hooded sweatshirts of their own or colorful jogging suits slowly paced the Promenade sorting through their personal weekend programs. A large droning sand cleaning machine ground meticulously through the beach. It rolled from jetty to jetty, and from the water to the seawall. It removed discarded sipping straws and cigarette butts from the otherwise pristine white sand. It had a bright spotlight on it, perhaps looking for people lying in the sand.

Chris related to Maurine that not long after Cape Island got the machine, it approached a young woman who was "involved" with a boyfriend beneath a sand colored blanket. The guy reacted and alertly dove out of the way; she could not. And in spite of its bright beam and overstated whirr was run over anyway. She lived to win a lawsuit. Subsequently, pedestrians were banned from the beach, after 11 p.m. "Apparently, folks can get involved with stuff and lose track of a cumbersome, illuminated, loud, municipally owned, sand-eating monster. Yeah right!" Chris said with doubt and finding humor in the situation. This episode was not the kind of publicity a resort sought or needed, having a vacationer shredded among the cigarette butts and discarded bottle caps. "But if one is dumb enough to ignore this thing, then they deserve to win the lawsuit!" He reasoned.

"Whatever the weather is going to do, I wish it would get here and get over with. I don't want my plane flying off into something crazy that we can't get out of," Maurine said, referring to the autumnal front moving toward land. The combination of the clattering of the sand-machine and the pounding surf possibly distorted Maurine's message.

"Before this 'hawk' chases us out of here, define for me what your 'new focus' means. I want to make sure that I hear what you are saying." Chris said, as he looked for Maurine to spell out how he might be involved in her plans.

"Are you asking me if you are part of my new focus?" Maurine questioned.

"Well put! Yeah, that is exactly what I am asking."

"Do you want to be?" She asked directly.

"Ever since I was sixteen-years-old! I have learned things about myself over the years, but I learned a long time ago that the one thing in this life I can do, is be happy with you. And I think I know how to make you happy. So hell yes, is my answer!" Chris roared above the breeze.

"So are you saying that you would rather live with me, than in your swanky digs at the Y?" Maurine kidded.

"Do you have a pool? The Y has a pool," he teased.

"No, but I bet you haven't learned how to swim anyway!"

"That was a trick question. I don't go into any water that is not the Atlantic Ocean. I just wanted to see if you would try to sell me. Good job! What a night!"

"If you look at the sky here or San Francisco, it is the same size. Wherever you stand, the stars will shine. However, I do not want to be under the stars unless you are with me, but I have to be out there. When are you coming?"

Chris's response was already prepared. He wanted to make sure what Maurine was asking, and said, "Let me finish out the month, which is about one week. I have to break it down to my parents, and that is going to be tough. It is time for me to become a grown-up, after all these years. I just don't want to drop what I am doing, come to California, and share the bed with you and your boyfriend.

He's probably some kind of jealous serial killer or something. Me personally, I'd have an ugly attitude with a new guy sleeping with my babe!"

"You tell me now that you are coming in October, and he is history. We are getting to the point that playing games are for kids. I am serious about you, and I am serious about wanting you with me. Is that clear enough for you?" Maurine exuberantly asked.

With the weather becoming increasingly more menacing, they cut short their viewing the moonlight reflecting off the ocean. The moon is now playing hide-and-seek behind the expanding clouds. They walked hand-in-hand toward the motel; a taboo for them years ago. Maurine made a point of passing the lot that used to be Joe's Tap; that used to be her home. She didn't make a big issue of it; she just wanted to take another look. About a block from the motel, the skies opened up for the first rainfall of the fall. By the time they reached their destination, they were thoroughly drenched but exceedingly ecstatic at their prospects. Chris spent the night with her, affirming the banishing of past demons.

Chapter Twenty-four *Omega*

Cape Island survived another hurricane season, and with it, two of its natives survived time's swirling whims. Chris and Maurine parted company to conclude shoring up life's loose ends. They were in their mid-teens when they last spoke with each other. After a couple of whirlwind days they rediscovered the energy they needed to complete the missing portions of their adult totality. And it was fun! Practically speaking, the town in which they both were raised, and from which they developed their values, had changed far more than they had. Sterling's sold its liquor license when it was revealed that the land it was built on was full of toxic refuse from a bygone era. The surrounding land had been a dumping ground for petroleum waste by-products since the early 1900s. These parcels had been directed to black people for a long time.

The entire section around Sterling's, a place where the black community resided, rested for decades atop buried drums of possible carcinogens. The playground that Chris had spent much of his early years playing Little League baseball, and later pick-up basketball games, had become Chernobylized, an environmental scourge. It was discovered to be a latent death trap as soil tests and ground water samples proved tainted with gunk. The anchor leg portion of removal of the minorities was completed without a whimper of protest. The biggest difference in relocating this group of displacements was they were getting a fairer payment for their property than those in the sixties and seventies, but they still had to go someplace else.

Sterling had been in negotiations with the city for a fair buy-out of the property. Although the city had given thought to condemning the property, and taking it as an eminent domain feature, they offered market value for the building and lot. Sterling declined, citing the city's offer was not what the property was worth. Private investors were scared out of the loop by the prospect of not knowing the extent of the contaminants. The city posed as the only suitable buyer. Despite the acknowledged poisons on the property, the city had visions of a new municipal complex with a city hall and library.

Although it seemed like they were taking a gamble, a private consortium with the influence and vision to recognize the strategic location for the property offered Sterling far more than the city did. This time he did not balk, and accepted the deal.

Cape Island offered only a limited number of liquor licenses, and until this one opened up, there were none available. There had not been one available for five years. This was a valuable credential.

Sterling's Silver Slipper Lounge closed its doors with a huge weekend bash prior to Halloween. The news was crushing. Cape Island did not have another business that catered to African-American clientele. Whether this concept was an indication of the great strides Cape Island had imprinted as a benchmark for free enterprise, or simply the culmination of a three-decade objective since the floods, to bleach the town white, one could not be sure. The critical element uncovered was that there were no black businesses of consequence left in the town.

Sterling's had served the area well. It lasted for twenty-three years. Jerry Strawberry worked there for the last six of those years, but was in severely ill health. The sale of the bar and the liquor license were far easier to reconcile, because of the contamination, than it was for the regulars of Sterling's to find another hangout. Once Joe's Tap was closed by the city, Sterling's had the exclusive attention of black social events. Now there was no favored place for the black community to kickback. That is to say what was left of the black community.

A phenomenon during the redevelopment of Cape May was the growing change of attitude, within the populace, regarding their environment. Everyone around Cape May knew they were running out of land. Worse than that, they were over-extending the capacities of their natural resources. Many of the new settlers came from urban or suburban centers with a serious concentration of buildings. Q-tip shaped cul-de-sacs, encircled by high-end houses within modern sub-divisions of similarly blueprinted, unimaginative, regurgitated likenesses, presented a standard thumbnail caricature of many of their home neighborhoods. The sense of nature had already been squeezed from the composition of that part their existence. Their harried lives had been balanced around the novelty of mobile phones, velcro, joysticks, Pac-Man, and IRA accounts. Once they embedded their initials on the shore community with their newly mortgaged structures, a need to lobby for referenda to discourage future building and growth emerged. The few remaining untouched tracts of green became sacred.

As these new tenants became comfortable with their accomplishments and surroundings, and reflected on their upwardly mobilized ascent, they scrambled to restrict others from disrupting the perimeter wildlife areas. Inland fishing, trapping, and crabbing that had been a part of the survival flow in past, had gradually ceded these open areas exclusively to the migrating birds. These tracts had become off-limits to builders and developers, thirty-some years after the ocean's major assault.

The Jersey shore fielded four seasons. The end of October is a defining time of year. From then until the late spring, the ardent beach visitors miss this gallery of color-coordinated scenery. The green trees of summer were blended onto an easel of gold, red, and orange, painting the landscape. Geese gather during this period on the freshwater ponds, as they head for warmer climates southward. Their flying V-formation, rehearsed for eons, provided the sound of autumn; their resonant honking cut through the misting mornings or the early darkness of the evening. This prompted, oddly enough, goose-bumps from their human witnesses. The temperatures dropped, dispelling any notions by the locals why they were not Florida or southern California, and blessed with year-round warmth. Raccoons poked their masked faces into the shivering nights. The lingering garden vegetables kept a wary eye out on the thermometer. The supple firmness of their luscious shapes awaited the season's first frost whence they were turned into mush on the vine. Yesterday they were laden with promise and strength; with a frost, they were transformed into zestless sponges of unrealized potential.

Chris had his ticket to California in his pocket. This was a ticket to uncap the lid on his unfulfilled life and potential. Maurine had Wil clean his stuff out, against his vehement protests. She smartly retained a lawyer to impose an injunction on him and deny his coming to her home or work. She opted not to go to church, for a while, reducing the "chance" of meeting him, although Wil had abdicated his membership in the church in the wake of the Sister Viola fiasco, a while ago.

Maurine allowed for a month to pass before she deemed the coast clear enough for Chris to come out. Wil could be a volatile lunatic with little nudging, and Maurine tried to combat that and put as much time and distance as she could between herself and him, before she lost Chris's momentum to come. The month of October proved just enough time for the air to clear, and for Maurine to bring Chris to San Francisco.

Wil moved to the house with his daughter and her family, which was not exactly a *Brady Bunch* reunion. He brooded and sulked and even called Maurine. He came to realize that she was not available for him to pursue. Although Wil absorbed a major shock to his fragile emotional system, he was smart enough to allow for Maurine's itinerary to play out, and did not interfere. He soon entered private therapy sessions hoping to remove the maiming personality scars that consistently marked him. In time, he did return to church with as much motivation as ever to clean up his uneven conduct. He sought a level of forgiveness and redemption for his outbursts and envy. He counseled with the minister, his former close friend, and Sister Viola's husband, as part of his therapy.

Sterling's contract with the city called for it to close on October 31, which was also Halloween. The thirty-first was on a Thursday, but Sterling's prepared for a continuous week-long going out of business bash from Thursday the 24th until they ran out of stock or they had to close the door at midnight on Thursday the 31st. Halloween seemingly brought out the inner-most emotions of the community. Although the situation was different from the Halloween night Joe was going to shoot Mo at Joe's Tap, change was heavy in the air. The significance of this Halloween would be a bombastic preamble to Chris's departure for San Francisco on Saturday November the 2nd.

As the news of Sterling's closing circulated, it was met with the same reception as the news of one's favorite dog getting run over by a car. It was not real family, and in time one can find another dog, or bar in which to hang out. But it was certainly going to take a long while to get over losing this one. In so many words, closing Sterling's was an awful, untimely tragedy.

Sterling's had a huge blowout on Saturday and Sunday before its closing. It was like a school reunion celebrating every class for the last twenty-three years. People came back from some far reaches to honor the last gasp of a commercial and social presence in the downsized version of the black section of town. Sterling's Silver Slipper Lounge still boasted an iconic vision of strength and promise. The reality of its fate had not fully seeped into consciousness. Its time was done undoubtedly long before it should have been.

The frost had come early and with it Sterling's had been reduced to a spongy likeness of itself. Chris's brother Stevie, a lawyer, and his sister Viv, a school guidance counselor came back not only to honor Sterling's closing, but to wish Chris a fond farewell. For Stevie and Viv, they hoped that Chris would find the happiness that had eluded him, but he probably never worked that hard to find. However, Stevie knew that Chris had always been hung-up on Maurine, and sensed that Chris had a good approach to making this work.

As Sterling was in the process of closing his doors, a funny thing happened on his way to a lucrative retirement. That day, that Halloween presented the East coast with the biggest nor'easter since the March '62 storm. Luckily for Sterling by the time it fully landed and flooded the area, the Silver Slipper Lounge was thoroughly out of stock and business life. This weather anomaly became known as the "perfect storm" and was made into a motion picture. But what this storm did was bracket a defining period that Cape Island amended its commercial and cultural objectives and buried the Other Cape May.

Sterling closed his door for the final time at midnight on Halloween. During its last week, Sterling's sold drinks at reduced prices and gave away almost anything else that was not nailed to the floor. By the end, Sterling's Silver Slipper Lounge stood as a gutted symbol, picked clean by the buzzards of greed, bureaucracy, and deception.

Sterling's departure left a gaping hole where just last week the parking lot was crowded and the music was rocking from inside the building, with the glittering foot lighted mural. It left a sizeable gap for the bridging of any inter-cultural expression for Cape May, for which there was still a need.

The irony associated with Sterling's, while it waited for the wrecking ball, was that for nearly thirty years the town sought to eliminate buildings in that part of the town. However, this move was regretted by all factions. The city lost on the image aspect of having black people living in a toxic sewer, and not letting on about it since the threatening refuse was buried there some sixty years before. Losing Sterling's as a tax ratable from somewhere other than the beach was also a blow. Plus the lighted sidewall was the first commercial indication that visitors saw when they hit town. And it sent the message that one could have fun in Cape May.

Chris left on his flight on Saturday, and met with Maurine in the early evening. She was radiant, and he was impressed with her reception of him. She stood in the airport with colorful mylar balloons filled with helium and a sign around her neck that said, "Welcome Chris!"

They settled into her condo. She had a couple of job interviews for him to go out on for Monday. But more than anything, they were happy to be together. He re-issued the medal to her that he had given her in 1964. It did not have quite the same impact as before, for Maurine had skeins of glittering chains, pendants and necklaces. She continued to wear the jewelry store gold and silver. With the pendants on the chain of one of her silver necklaces, she added the tatty brown-silver second place medal. It was not only for the sentimental remembrances for the days gone by, but she told Chris that it was saving a place in her heart for when he got her the *ring*.

Sterling's Silver Slipper Lounge was cleaned out and vacated in the same week that Chris was finding his way around San Francisco. Maurine taught him how to use the streetcars and the buses. Chris was hired the same week he arrived there. Maurine got him a job with a newly founded computer company, as a salesman. Chris had a six week training course to deal with, but computers seemed like a field that might be going somewhere in 1991. He would purchase his new car with its obligatory new car payment, once he started in the field, and out of the office. Chris neither found the time to become homesick, nor lose sleep over the woman he saw when he lived in Philly.

Maurine never yearned for Wil's barking at her. Her liquor cabinet was not addressed with the voracity that had been the case when Wil lived there. She would have some wine with her evening meal, and would have all of *one* Long Island tea when she had a night of socializing. The threat of settling her life in the dregs of endless bottles of alcohol never materialized. However, that image would quietly guide her when drinking was part of the atmosphere. Both Maurine and Chris looked to the future through a rose-colored telescope lens.

Epilogue

The world around Cape May flourished in the Victorian trappings that it began polishing in the sixties. The effects of weather had lifted the resort to a status of regional and perhaps national prominence. As the century marched to a close, and thus closing out a millennium, Cape May stood strong. An enterprising businessman, dealing from merely a position of nostalgia of days gone by, brought back to life in a limited way, a train coming into Cape May. The range of the train's excursions was for a few miles, and offered a sightseeing view that wasn't on a bicycle or in a horse-drawn carriage.

Drunkenness still found accessible haunts in Cape May. There were fewer blacks, and far fewer Hispanics in the town than in the fifties and sixties. Fights triggered by racial differences had more of a history than a future. There was too much invested by all parties to do much fighting. Alcohol traditionally had a way of allowing skin color to be perceived with a more confrontational acuity. Overt racism in town was devalued by the immense prices for property. If one can afford to buy the house, or pay the rents, so be it! Money was the abiding king of the community.

Maurine and Chris settled their lives in San Francisco. Chris became an executive for the computer company that he entered on the ground floor as a salesman when he first arrived. Maurine became the magazine's editor when her predecessor moved on to a national magazine. Her schedule was hectic but she doted on her time with Chris. She implemented marketing changes at the magazine and expanded its sales base. She picked Chris's mind on varied subject matter for her editorials. Some of his "revolutionary" readings from the late sixties, albeit piecemeal; found their way into the women's magazine.

They borrowed time from the busy schedules they both had, and came back home for a personal matter. They got married in 1994. They had their wedding at Chris's family church in Cape May. Chris's church had recently been given a grant to refurbish its exterior. It was a sizable amount of money that was extended through the auspices of "urban renewal." The church built a century before, was a Victorian structure and qualified as a historic landmark.

That church had also undergone an internal identity face-lift of sorts over the years. When Chris was a child, he had gone to the Methodist church that had an entrenched black congregation. It was the recently retired minister from this church who performed the wedding ceremony at Joe's Tap, nearly 25 years before. In the 1980s, this church shared its minister with the traditionally white Methodist church. In the nineties, the churches merged into the same building, dispensing of any racial divide. The national and local social climate had warmed to such a point, and the number of black worshipers had lessened, making two churches financially unsound. Older black church members objected to this union on the basis of tradition and heritage, but there was little to offer that would stave off this merger. Cape May offered more inter-cultural opportunities.

The resilience of that community, "the Other Cape May," over some trying times, provided for one heroic effort without that player even knowing it. Maurine's determination to put distance between herself and a Dickens-like upbringing was a tribute to her capacity to seek a personal level of accomplishment. There were a number of setbacks, but she would not let them impede her growth or undermine her ambition.

Maurine's record collection was once potent with sentiment and hope, but those who had influenced that sentiment were gone. Maurine finally called Elmo's vending company to touch base with him, when she came home for her wedding. She hoped that he could come to it. She was stunned to learn that Elmo had died in 1992, not long after the recovery of the collection. Elmo's son ran the vending company and told her that he died of natural causes at age sixty-six.

Helena York still swapped Christmas cards with Maurine, but there was no mystique to the relationship. Helena's family came and participated in the wedding. With no one left to identify with the collection, Maurine sold her records for $15,000. This was an act that took her much soul-searching to achieve. She simply came to a business decision to make the sale.

With those proceeds, coupled with Mo's insurance benefit, Maurine and Chris built an eight-unit apartment building on the corner where the little store brought them together thirty years before. The store was long gone, but the feeling that Chris and Maurine wanted to preserve, glistened from that corner. They cherished their not-so-annual visits back home. They kept one unit available for their infrequent visits to Cape Island. Maurine had vowed that the record collection was not about money, but its sale cemented a financial toehold for Maurine and Chris in their hometown. In that all of the individuals were dead that could be associated with the records, Maurine and Chris still had a lot of life ahead of them and appreciated the opportunity to invest in their home and heritage. In so many ways, the record collection had practically and sentimentally advanced into the apartment building.

Upon the advent of the 21st century Cape May stood sparkling and inviting, fortified against nature's wrath, and wooing visitors to its overbooked inns and hotels. However, of all of the old-time regulars who contributed to the personality of Joe's Tap, none saw the new millennium. Puerto Rican Jesus retired from the school and died peacefully with his wife and four of his six children at his bedside, at age sixty-eight. Doc died of the same liver condition that claimed his buddy Jinx, at sixty-seven. Big Dick was besieged with an intestinal cancer and died. He weighed 135 pounds, half of his normal size, at the time of his death; he was seventy-eight. Jerry Strawberry died of a mysterious ailment at age forty-eight. He died before he got a chance to look for another job after Sterling's closed. Some say it was Agent Orange that struck him down; others claim it was AIDS, brought about by administering dirty needles during his drug-tainted time in Cape

May. This was a significant portion of his life. Then there were others who suggested Jerry Strawberry was a homosexual. Sterling's regulars noted that he did not chase women or have a girlfriend after Mary's death. They inferred that he swore off women after his time with Mary, for whatever the reason. AIDS, in the eighties and nineties, was just as incurable as polio had been in the early fifties. Jerry Strawberry was the youngest to die from the cadre of the Joe's Tap regulars.

After Sterling's closed, many former patrons looked for new drinking spots. For Bertha, it was the casinos. She never took root in Sterling's as it was. Somehow she never approved of the moniker "Miss Bertha" that the youngish clientele called her in Sterling's. She noted that it was respectful sounding but it also had an implied condescension. For Bertha, peer acceptance carried more weight than being seen as an "elder statesperson" in Sterling's, around kids who were barely old enough to buy liquor. There was no one around to call her "Bertha Bertha."

The casinos pampered older people, and Bertha approved of the attention her age brought from there. Sometimes she would take Susie to the casinos. Bertha died when her car skid off the road in a severe rainstorm while she was returning from visiting a casino in Atlantic City. Ironically, her accident occurred the same night Chris and Maurine reunited and were chased from the Promenade by the weather. Bertha was by herself. Her blood alcohol level was .17%, well above the legal limit for intoxication. She was seventy-seven.

Poison Sumac outlived her husband, his girlfriend, three of her five children, and Bertha Bertha. Susie McHendry passed without having a firm grasp on her sanity. Her demise accelerated when Bertha died. She died in a nursing home a couple years after Bertha passed. Her death was a perfect-storm combination of old age, despair, dementia and alcoholism. In her last years, she had few visitors and funerals for her children proved her only activity outside of her residence. She died at age seventy-nine.

In seeking the utopian resort, Cape May lost the small town feel for family and community. The image of the town was reshaped by the weather and redirected fiscal ideals. When the high school moved in the early sixties it took with it an identity on which the city had thrived. The kids had frequented the area ice cream shops and purchased bicycles from the bike shop that was across the street from the school. The departed high school had provided a cultural haven for the community. During the transition, the loss of the high school band marching through town on a football Saturday was just another negative the town absorbed. It is said that a city without a high school is a city without a soul.

Once the business hub, Washington Street was a focal point for purchasing everyday staples and maybe provided the opportunity of seeing a popular movie there. Until the mid-1960s, Washington Street was really a street with automobiles motoring through in two directions. The street itself was removed and re-paved to create a walking mall. The mall offered outdoor restaurants and pubs, soft ice cream outlets, and kids handing out free samples of fudge, trying to tempt over-weight diabetics into buying a pound of that stuff. A bowling alley, pool hall, a couple banks, a movie theater, supermarkets, drug stores, a dentist office, gas stations, car dealerships and clothing stores all got swallowed up by progress. This does not even mention the businesses on either side of the train station. The coal yard rested on one side and the Western Union office was on the other. Chances are their days were numbered anyway. Washington Street went from a community center where people knew each other to a tourist attraction with folks coming from all over the world to visit and then leave when their room reservations expired.

The raids by speculating profiteers left the city reeling with a vacuum of grass roots thinking. The childish banter concerning grown-up concepts died on the vine about the time Joe's Tap was bulldozed into history. Perspectives from those alcohol-laden savants at Joe's, who held court for so long, really did provide an alternative thought process. Sometimes they even made sense. Other businesses were lost in the shuffle during that period, as well. However, few of those places provided the multi-ethnic sanctuary that Joe's Tap did. Cape Island has missed Joe's Tap or at the least, a place like it. Its time and its place have come and gone. A resurgent emanation is all but impossible, but for its time and its place there was nothing like Joe Tap, and the grit of little girl who survived it.

Printed in the United States
By Bookmasters